"I want

She stared at him, wondering if she'd heard him correctly. She also wondered exactly when her desire for him had become so transparent.

"Why?" she asked, then promptly regretted even opening her mouth.

"Do I need a reason?" he said quietly.

"No," she whispered.

"Would you prefer it if I didn't touch you?"

"I want you to hold me."

"Elizabeth . . ." he groaned.

She paused, searching his features. "Did I say something wrong?"

"Not wrong. Never wrong. It's just that I've wondered since that first night what it would be like to hold you in my arms. I need to know, Elizabeth. I really need to know."

WHAT ARE *LOVESWEPT* ROMANCES?

They are stories of true romance and touching emotion. We believe those two very important ingredients are constants in our highly sensual and very believable stories in the LOVE-SWEPT line. Our goal is to give you, the reader, stories of consistently high quality that may sometimes make you laugh, sometimes make you cry, but are always fresh and creative and contain many delightful surprises within their pages.

Most romance fans read an enormous number of books. Those they truly love, they keep. Others may be traded with friends and soon forgotten. We hope that each LOVESWEPT romance will be a treasure—a "keeper." We will always try to publish

LOVE STORIES YOU'LL NEVER FORGET
BY AUTHORS YOU'LL ALWAYS REMEMBER

The Editors

Loveswept ® 765

LONESOME TONIGHT

LAURA TAYLOR

BANTAM BOOKS
NEW YORK · TORONTO · LONDON · SYDNEY · AUCKLAND

LONESOME TONIGHT

A Bantam Book / November 1995

*If you would be interested in receiving protective vinyl covers for your
Loveswept books, please write to this address for information:*

Loveswept
Bantam Books
P.O. Box 985
Hicksville, NY 11802

ISBN 0-553-44510-3

Published simultaneously in the United States and Canada

*Bantam Books are published by Bantam Books, a division of Bantam Dou-
bleday Dell Publishing Group, Inc. Its trademark, consisting of the words
"Bantam Books" and the portrayal of a rooster, is Registered in U.S.
Patent and Trademark Office and in other countries. Marca Registrada.
Bantam Books, 1540 Broadway, New York, New York 10036.*

PRINTED IN THE UNITED STATES OF AMERICA

OPM   0 9 8 7 6 5 4 3 2 1

This book is dedicated to the women writers
who helped me find my way back
into the light:

Debbi Wood, Jan Ference, Rosanne
Falcone, Kathleen Creighton, Helen Myers,
Deborah Smith, Alex Thorleifson, Peggy
Webb, and Diane Chamberlain.

I thank each of them for their love and
support during a very painful time
in my life.

I would also like to take this opportunity to
acknowledge the guidance and information
provided during the writing of this book by
two special friends:

Pat Vergne, Lieutenant of Lifeguards, City
of Del Mar, California,
and
Bruce Stine, San Jose Police Department,
San Jose, California.

ONE

Michael Cassidy made his way along the ribbon of sand that edged the Southern California coastline with a single-mindedness typical of his personality. He ignored the waves surging against the shore and flirting with the tips of his crutches. He no longer heard the lone gull that screeched overhead. And if he noticed the setting sun, an electric-pink sphere, there wasn't even the faintest acknowledgment in his angular features.

Other than an occasional blink to dislodge the beads of sweat trickling into his eyes, Michael's gaze remained fixed. He labored forward without a thought to the curious image he presented to residents of the cottages, condos, and million-dollar compounds lining the beach.

Working past the pain of protesting muscles, Michael gripped the handles of his crutches and used his uninjured leg like a rudder, driving himself at a relentless pace until he finally ran out of hard-packed sand.

Once he circled the huge boulder at the foot of the Torrey Pines cliffs, he undertook the return three-mile journey to Seagrove Park.

Sweat spiked his short-cropped, dark auburn hair, streaked his tanned skin, and saturated the running shorts and faded USC Film School T-shirt he wore. The muscle ticking high in his left cheek and his gritted teeth hinted at the cost of his exertion, but he refused to admit to himself that six weeks spent babying a badly torn Achilles tendon had done little more than remind him that his forty-year-old body—even if it was the well-maintained body of a former triathlete—needed time to mend.

Although he'd spent the previous week testing his endurance with shorter trips up and down the beach, this was his toughest workout so far. He was functioning on raw nerves by the time he spotted the beachfront park. Once there, he halted, struggling momentarily to maintain his balance. He gulped oxygen, sucking it into his burning lungs as fast as he could manage the task.

Michael savored each and every stroke of the cool breeze that washed over his skin. The setting sun now captured and held his attention. It brought to mind a documentary film he'd directed at a West African orphanage in the early years of his career. The sunsets he'd witnessed during that particular shoot had been nothing short of miraculous. None until now, he realized, had been capable of rivaling Mother Nature at her most splendid.

Michael frowned suddenly, his appreciation of the dramatic view displaced in the space of a single heartbeat by the sight of a raven-haired woman clad in an unadorned white tank-style bathing suit as she emerged from the advancing tide. He froze, immobilized by what he saw. Was she the product of some endorphin-induced fantasy caused by too much exercise? He blinked, then refocused. She didn't disappear. She moved steadily toward him, slicking her shoulder-length hair back from her face, then smoothing the moisture from her eyes and cheeks with the tips of her fingers. He watched her fight to maintain her footing when an incoming wave crashed into her. She smiled suddenly, her expression a mixture of pleasure and triumph when she succeeded in remaining upright.

Michael felt the air leave his lungs. The muscles that mapped his torso and long limbs quivered. Heat flooded his bloodstream, transforming it into rivers of flame. He realized then that she was the most seductive sight he'd seen in years.

Like most strong men, Michael exerted an extraordinary amount of control over himself both personally and professionally. He exercised that control now, employing it with a ruthlessness that wasn't at all foreign to his nature. He didn't want to frighten this woman, nor did he want to lose her now that he'd found her. Rocked by his final thought, Michael Cassidy stopped thinking altogether and simply indulged his senses.

Elizabeth Parker burst free of a towering wave just seconds before it collapsed onto itself. After skirting the suction of the dangerous undertow, she moved through the water with a level of skill that reflected her many years of experience as an ocean swimmer. A California native and coastal resident for every one of her thirty-four years, she savored both the challenge and the peace of mind she derived from swimming.

She surrendered to the powerful swells, allowing them to propel her slender body forward. Her thoughts drifted as she glided toward the shoreline, but she remained aware of her surroundings, biding her time until the ideal moment. She surged upward without warning, staggered under the impact of several breaking waves, and then fought to remain standing in the swirling water and shifting sand. She finally gained her footing, setting as her next goal the towel she'd left on the stretch of empty beach that separated the Pacific from Seagrove Park.

Elizabeth finger-combed her thick dark hair out of her face. Her eyes adjusted to the dusky shadows that had begun to consume the beachfront during her swim. She paused in the knee-deep surf the instant she noticed the man braced on crutches. He stood only a few feet from the water's edge.

Elizabeth searched his angular facial features for hints about his character. What she saw as she studied him intrigued her—a conservative haircut, thick eyebrows, expressive hazel eyes with crow's feet fanning into the hairline, a strong nose, and finally, a sturdy jaw.

At first glance his muscular body suggested that he was in his early thirties, but his eyes—shadowed eyes that revealed a weariness of spirit that she recognized more easily than she would have wished—prompted her to speculate that his fortieth birthday was behind him. She shifted her gaze past his crutches, her attention lingering on the bandage swathing his left ankle and foot. Her instincts insisted that he wasn't just another surfer who'd tangled with a bad wave. This man looked more—Elizabeth searched for just the right words—*substantial* and *complex* than the typical wave-chasers who populated the local beaches.

As she measured his tall, powerful-looking frame against her smaller, five-foot-four-inch body, she decided that his injury and her self-defense training put them on a par physically. She also thought she recognized him, but until she established his identity to her satisfaction, she erred on the side of good judgment and kept her distance. Elizabeth Parker knew far too much about human nature not to be cautious.

As she met his gaze again, she acknowledged his perusal of her for what it appeared to be on the surface —simple male curiosity about a woman. Nothing more, nothing less. She realized then that she didn't mind his inspection. Hers, after all, had been just as thorough. The only thing she really minded was the chilly breeze blowing in off the Pacific, a common occurrence that often surprised visitors to the area at the end of a warm summer day.

Noticing the scar above his left eyebrow, she concluded that the mark added a certain recklessness to his appearance. He couldn't be called handsome, not by any stretch of the imagination. He looked sturdy and rugged. And much to her relief, he wasn't attired in the latest designer athletic wear so typical of a community often referred to as Hollywood South. Clad instead in shorts and a faded T-shirt, he seemed unpretentious, even a little rough around the edges.

She saluted him for the absence of gold chains around his neck. Nothing turned her off more. A woman friend had once commented that she had very plebian taste in men. Elizabeth inwardly smiled as she recalled the observation. In truth, she tended to measure most men against the standard set by her father and brothers. She knew them to be dependable men who could laugh at themselves, fair-minded men, even when they failed to understand some of the difficult choices she'd been forced to make in recent years. Real men. She wasn't certain exactly how she knew it, but she sensed that this man might be more real than most.

"Hello," Elizabeth finally said as she glanced at the towel she'd left in the sand. "You startled me."

She caught the flash of shock in his eyes before he blinked it away. She almost smiled, but she managed not to. She understood the cause of his reaction. She knew her voice was unusual. Men, especially men who didn't know her, often mistook it as a seductive come-on, while those who knew her well realized that like her mother and sister, she had little control over a sultry sound reminiscent of the finest aged whiskey.

"Then we're even, because you surprised me. I thought I was alone." He nodded in the direction of the towel on the sand between them. "Yours?" he asked as he continued his intense perusal of her face and figure.

"Mine," Elizabeth confirmed.

He speared the length of white terry with the tip of one crutch while balancing his weight on his good ankle. He extended the towel to her, but made no overt moves in her direction.

She gave him an A plus in the common-sense department. Stepping forward, she reached out, snagged the towel with her fingertips, and shook the sand from it, but she stayed in the ankle-deep surf. "Thank you."

"My pleasure."

She dried her face, arms, and thighs, still regarding him with a curious gaze. He gave no sign that he was uncomfortable with her scrutiny. He simply returned the favor with an honesty that suggested he had nothing to hide. She hoped that was the case. "Other than the early-morning hours, I think this is my favorite time at the beach."

"Do you mind sharing it?" he asked.

His voice, she decided, was the voice of a man who knew his way around women. Oddly enough, that didn't frighten her. But instead of reacting to the seductive sound or to the unexpected feelings it stirred deep within, she laughed at his question as she fastened the towel saronglike at her hips. "Not at all. Paradise should always be shared."

"Do you usually swim alone?"

Elizabeth heard the sharp edge in his words despite the noise of the waves tumbling behind her. "Usually," she admitted, her wariness returning. "Why?"

"It strikes me as dangerous, that's all."

"Would it ease your mind to know that I spent several years here as a lifeguard?"

He didn't answer right away. Instead, he gave her question a moment of obvious thought as his eyes swept over the contours of her slender body. Not an impulsive man, Elizabeth realized. She liked that quality in him too.

"Not really, but it's your call."

She relaxed somewhat. "You're right. It is." Her pleasant expression softened the impact of her words, but her tone contained enough firmness to convey the message that she meant them. "I have an enormous amount of respect for the power of Mother Nature."

"Then I'll respect your judgment."

She inclined her head, certain at that instant that he rarely offered respect or anything else to total strangers. She couldn't help wondering, albeit briefly, why those closest to her weren't capable of doing the same. Casting aside the thought, she said, "I think we're neighbors."

A siren screamed in the distance, as if to punctuate her remark. She flinched, her attention straying to the streetlights twinkling beyond the beach. Even paradise, she reminded herself, required vigilant protectors. She had once been one of the most vigilant, but a stranger and fate had robbed her of her dreams.

He moved unexpectedly. Elizabeth's gaze swung back to him, her concern spiking until she noticed that he'd simply shifted backward in the sand. She wanted to believe, she realized, that hearing the siren had encouraged him to demonstrate that he didn't pose a threat to her.

Although the expression on his face indicated that

he'd noted her heightened wariness, he simply asked, "Do you live here year-round?"

She nodded. "And you're visiting?" She waited for him to reveal what she already suspected.

"That's right. Hal and Diane Buckman lent me their place for the rest of the summer."

"Then we *are* neighbors, at least for the duration of your stay." The Buckmans, like many others who owned second homes in Del Mar, were a part of the moneyed Hollywood elite who had carved out niches for themselves in the beach community many years earlier. She assumed that he was a part of that elite, although she didn't recognize him as a film star. Perhaps he was a writer or a producer. Her instincts still guiding her, she stepped out of the low surf and extended her hand. "I'm Elizabeth Parker."

He offered his hand in return, maintaining his balance on the crutches with practiced ease. "Michael Cassidy."

She accepted his handshake, but his touch roused unexpected sensations within her, warmly intimate sensations that prompted her to tug free of him after just a brief moment of contact. Something rushed into her bloodstream despite her withdrawal, something hot and quite startling. Unable to conceal her response, Elizabeth trembled.

He frowned. "You're chilled, aren't you?"

She felt hot and cold, but she didn't intend to admit that fact to a man she didn't know. "Not really. I'm used to the evening breeze." She forced a smile to her lips. "It tends to surprise the tourists though."

He chuckled. "Somehow, I think that pleases you."

Elizabeth shrugged, his insight rousing her interest in him even more. "It makes distinguishing between the locals and visitors fairly easy."

"Your point has merit."

"I'm glad you think so," she quipped, enjoying his dry humor.

"I need to get back. If you don't mind walking at a snail's pace, I'd welcome your company."

"Lead the way," she encouraged.

He turned, careful not to let the loose sand trip him up as he got under way. Elizabeth walked along beside him, her initial worry about his motives fading even more as a companionable silence emerged between them. Taken at face value, Michael Cassidy was simply an appealing man on crutches.

Still, she knew from experience that real jeopardy, whether emotional or physical, was often quite subtle at the outset. A sigh escaped her before she could mute the sound. Would she ever stop remembering what her former fiancé had done? she wondered. Would she ever be able to trust a man again? She felt Michael's curious gaze, and she silently applauded his restraint when he didn't intrude on her thoughts. Elizabeth loathed explaining her past to anyone, least of all to a stranger.

They passed several elegant homes and a beachfront restaurant. She sidestepped an abandoned beach chair, closing the space that separated them as they walked along. "You've been on those cruthes for a while now, haven't you?"

"Six weeks and two days."

"What happened?"

He cast a chagrined look in her direction. "I zigged when I should have zagged. Pure clumsiness on my part. The good news is that the situation's not permanent."

"Inconvenient though. I've done my time on those sticks. Hated every minute of it. You've obviously survived the housebound-and-cranky stage," she speculated with a relaxed smile.

He chuckled. "Just barely, but I suspect I've managed to alienate most of my friends since the accident happened."

She laughed at his admission. "Let me guess. A torn Achilles tendon?"

"Unfortunately."

"The healing time can be very unpredictable."

"Tell me about it."

"Not fun," she commiserated. "But you look tough enough to handle the challenge."

"I'm bored out of my mind."

"You picked a great spot to be bored though."

"I can't disagree, and I'm grateful that Hal and Diane were willing to lend me their place."

"I lifeguarded with their oldest daughter when we were both in college. I still run into them periodically. They're nice people."

"Very nice. I've known them for several years too." He paused suddenly, grimacing as he straightened his leg and rested his cast-encased foot atop a partially buried length of driftwood.

Glancing his way, Elizabeth hesitated. The light

shining from a beachfront restaurant illuminated his sudden pallor. "Problem?"

"Fatigue and a cramp," he gritted out as he reached down to massage the calf area of his healthy leg. "I pushed it too hard tonight."

She gave him high marks for his honesty. "My crystal ball tells me that you went all the way to the cliffs on those crutches. Then you turned around and made the return trip."

Surprise mingled with the strain already etched into his features as he straightened and peered at her. "Guilty. How'd you know?"

"I did it once when I was on crutches," she admitted.

"Why?"

"I'd broken my ankle. I was testing myself."

He nodded. "I understand. You were an athlete?"

His gaze lingered on the swell of her breasts before his eyes returned to her face. Instead of taking offense, her pulse picked up speed, and she was glad for the semidarkness that concealed the flush spreading over her skin. She realized with some surprise that his admiration didn't alarm her. She actually liked it.

Clearing her throat, Elizabeth forced her attention away from his rugged features and back to his question. "Just moderately athletic. At the time of my self-initiated marathon, I was trying to prove a point to one of my brothers."

"Did you?"

She laughed. "Hardly. He left me in his dust."

"You don't seem to mind."

"Big brother was determined to teach me to use my head when my body wasn't willing to cooperate. I learned an important lesson about boundary lines that day."

"I read you loud and clear," Michael said, his tone wry.

She shrugged. "The timing on any injury is never good."

He looked at her for a moment. "You aren't afraid of me."

His comment came at her like an unanticipated body blow, and Elizabeth felt every bit of the tension that suddenly infused her. Her smile faded, her normally animated face and sparkling dark eyes becoming a blank canvas. "That's an odd thing to say."

"Just an observation. You started sizing me up the moment you spotted me. Your body language was nothing short of amazing. So was the expression on your face. Most people don't pull it together that fast."

She asked ever so softly, "Should I be afraid of you, Michael Cassidy?" She didn't care that he looked shocked. She wanted an answer.

"Never," he insisted.

"Then why say something like that to me?"

"I honestly wasn't trying to frighten you. It's just that speaking to a stranger can be risky."

"Talking to anyone you don't know in this day and age is a risk, but I'm not so paranoid that I'm going to stop living."

"You seem more streetwise than most women," he remarked. "You aren't easily intimidated, are you?"

She didn't attempt to conceal her disbelief. "By the look on your face, I don't need to tell you how sexist that sounded."

"Guilty, once again," he conceded.

Elizabeth hid the smile his lack of remorse prompted. "Being aware of my environment is second nature to me, and not surprising since—" She paused, the reflex to refer to herself as a police officer a painful reminder that her law enforcement career was a part of the past. ". . . Not at all surprising since my dad and my brothers are cops."

"That explains it."

She thought he sounded as if he'd just solved a puzzle, and she felt some of her inner tension drain away. "Unless you're planning to knock me on the head for the purse I'm obviously not carrying, we don't have a problem. Besides, I suspect that a quick getaway might be a major problem for you."

"I'm not into purses or assault."

His deadpan expression made her laugh, and the sound resembled a throaty caress. "That's reassuring."

"Remarkable sound."

"So I've been told," she admitted, her eyes shifting away from him.

"I meant your laughter," he shot back, as though to say he didn't make a habit of commenting on something as obvious as a woman's voice. "Although I have to admit that your voice is nothing short of extraordinary."

"All the women in my family sound like me."

He peered at her for a moment before speaking.

The expression on his face made Elizabeth's insides thrum. Unsettled by her reaction, she looked away, but her heart raced wildly.

"Most men get lost in the sound, don't they? They can't get past their idea of what they want you to be, and they fail to make the transition to the woman who's speaking. I'll bet they also miss out on what you're really saying to them."

She nodded, pleased and unexpectedly relieved by his willingness to see her as a whole person, not simply as a sound or a body.

"Did you know that the right woman's voice has the power to make a man's soul ache?"

Shocked by his question and the intimacy that seemed to resonate in his low tone, she held her breath for a moment and searched his features for sincerity. She had an unexpected need for him to be different from the men she'd known in the past. Especially one man, a man who'd been unwilling, along with her family, to respect the most painful decision she'd ever made in her life.

Despite her uncertainty, and the fact that she'd never before engaged in quite such a conversation with a man she'd just met, Elizabeth refused to back away from his remark. If anything, she felt compelled to confront it—and him—head-on. "A man needs to be wise enough to listen to the words that aren't spoken aloud. Important messages are conveyed in a variety of ways."

"Reading minds is tough work."

"Ignoring the obvious is unwise," she countered.

"Anyway, I'm talking about really listening, not clair-voyance."

"I'll need to remember that if we're going to be friends, won't I?"

She froze, not certain how to respond to his question. Fantasizing about a man was one thing, but inviting a virtual stranger into her world was something else altogether.

Michael waited, his intent study of her facilitated by the glow of floodlights from the public parking lot adjacent to the beach. "If friendship is possible, Elizabeth Parker."

She met his gaze, refusing to be coy. That particular tactic, especially when dealing with the male gender, had never suited her. It didn't now. "Friendship is possible," she confirmed, "but it takes time and I have rules. I won't be used or manipulated."

"You say precisely what you mean, don't you?"

"Always. I'm a very direct person."

"Most people aren't."

"Most people play word games. I don't. Not ever. Life is complicated enough."

"Too much honesty can be a double-edged sword."

"It's the only way I'm willing to live."

Michael jerked a nod in her direction, but he said nothing more. Elizabeth wondered about the nerve she'd apparently hit, but she didn't press him for an explanation. She watched instead as he resumed his trek up the beach. The rippling strength of his decidedly masculine anatomy sent her imagination on a collision course with desires never really appeased by the man she'd almost married.

As she matched Michael's stride, Elizabeth reminded herself that impulsive behavior wasn't her style. She listened for a moment to the inner voice that urged her to eliminate this man as a potential candidate for friendship. He was an unknown quantity, a potential wild card in the deck of life. An honest woman, she sensed that she was destined for failure.

Something—she didn't know exactly what—about Michael Cassidy drew her closer. It didn't seem to matter that she had a very busy life, her days at the university full, her nights occupied by study, and her recent past a mine field that still contained undetonated shells. An advanced degree in counseling didn't just happen, and she knew she needed to focus on the goals she'd set for herself as she embarked on a new career. But other needs, more personal needs long neglected, thrived within her too, even if considering them meant taking emotional risks she hadn't anticipated.

They passed several brightly lighted residences, a restaurant with a full patio of diners, and group of young people gathered around a firepit. Laughter, conversation, and music spilled into the night air and mated with the subtler sounds of the incoming tide. Elizabeth didn't feel inclined to fill the silence they shared as they walked. It was comfortable, and so unlike the awkward lapses in conversation she'd experienced with men in the past.

Her footsteps slowed a few moments later, the unmanned 19th Street lifeguard tower drawing her gaze.

A halo of lights strung along the rooftop railing shone brightly in the encroaching darkness. She recalled with pleasure the summers she'd spent stationed at the tower, summers during which she'd performed ocean rescues, cared for temporarily misplaced children, employed first aid skills, and taught swimming to locals and visitors, young and old.

He slowed his pace. "Is this where you worked as a lifeguard?"

"Yes."

"Good memories?"

"Very good memories," Elizabeth confirmed. "I miss the simplicity of those days."

"Things tend to be simpler when you have your life ahead of you," he said.

She shivered, reflecting for a moment on his comment, then setting it aside. She'd once believed that life was simple, but then things had grown so complex that she'd lost her way for a time. She suddenly sensed Michael Cassidy's grasp of complex life problems and even more complex solutions as she hurried past the three remaining homes that stood between the tower and her cottage. A part of her appreciated his response, but another part of her—the part that had retreated when she'd been let down by those she'd once trusted with her fragile emotions—felt the need to deflect it. Elizabeth told herself that she neither wanted nor needed a stranger's compassion, even though the absence of compassion from her family still deeply wounded her.

Did she want Michael Cassidy to be a kindred

spirit? she wondered. Elizabeth dismissed the thought an instant later, because she knew it didn't really matter. They were like the proverbial ships that passed in the night. Nothing would come of this encounter, she told herself. Nothing at all. Grappling with the regret she felt as she paused in front of her recently restored cottage, she said a silent prayer of thanks for the darkness that hid her very mixed emotions.

"Thanks for keeping me company."

"You're welcome. Perhaps we'll run into each other again," she said, trying to sound upbeat when she suddenly felt anything but that.

He stiffened, then took a lingering moment to ponder her remark. Feeling like a fool, Elizabeth held her breath while he tried to make out her features in the semidarkness.

"Sounds doubtful," he finally said.

She exhaled. "My schedule's unpredictable."

He nodded. "I understand."

His tone of voice said he understood far too much, but that still didn't make an explanation possible, so she didn't provide one. "Take care of yourself, Michael." Turning, she started toward the low retaining wall that surrounded the beach side of her small home.

"Ditto, Elizabeth."

The regret she heard in his voice as he said her name made her hesitate. It seemed so genuine, as did his apparent willingness to accept the barrier she'd just erected between them. She took his behavior as a sign of respect, and looked back over her shoulder at him.

"The Buckmans have an antique cowbell hanging beside the gate to their back patio. You've probably noticed it. If you find yourself in a crisis, the neighbors are conditioned to respond to it."

"I'm not helpless, dammit!"

Although she heard his flaring temper, it didn't bother her. She understood the cause, even felt empathy for him. "I suspect that you're one of the least helpless people on the planet."

"Sorry. I'm not used to this," Michael said, his frustration replaced by a matter-of-fact tone of voice laced with steel. "I hate it."

Emotions too diverse to name flooded her heart. She fought the urge to comfort him. "I really do understand. Being dependent is humbling. It's a painful reminder that we're all vulnerable at one time or another in our lives."

He exhaled, the sound raw. She sensed that he was grappling with more than an out-of-commission ankle, but then, so was she. Reminding herself that she didn't get paid to rescue people any longer, Elizabeth stepped over the low wall. His silence made her hesitate, and she let herself glance his way one last time. A perfect, bright white moon outlined his tall, muscular body and the crutches that kept him upright.

"Be well, Michael Cassidy," she said, her voice more distinctive than usual thanks to the confusing emotions coursing through her. She allowed herself to wonder, then, what it would feel like to be held by this man—this man who was a stranger, this man who struck her as capable of seducing her heart if she gave him the opportunity. She suddenly ached to know precisely what it would feel like to experience his embrace and his passion.

"You too, Elizabeth Parker. You too."

TWO

Intimate strangers.

The phrase emerged without warning from Michael's subconscious as he watched Elizabeth step over the low retaining wall, and it lingered in his mind as she made her way to the rear deck of the one-story cottage she called home.

She hesitated, then glanced his way, but only for the briefest of moments. The relief he felt when she paused shocked him. It also sent the breath he'd been holding from his body in a heavy gust.

She'd spoken to him as well. The sound of his name as it passed her lips provoked an unexpected ache of pure longing within his soul. He answered her, but the polite words were a far cry from what he really wanted to say.

Michael didn't speak again. Unsettled by the emotional need and raw hunger she inspired, he watched her open the back door of the small dwelling with the key suspended from the long silver chain she wore around her neck. He saw her hesitate once more. In the end, though, she didn't look back. She squared her shoulders, slipped into the cottage, and eased the door shut.

Michael sensed that she intended to avoid him during the remainder of his stay at the beach. He hated that their time together was over, but he didn't intend to push the woman into a corner. Not simply for the obvious reasons, but because he resented it when anyone crowded him. He silently vowed not to subject Elizabeth Parker to that kind of performance pressure. Not ever.

Regret and desire continued to resonate within him though. He tried to banish the feeling by the sheer force of his will, but he failed. Tightening his grip on his crutches, he forced himself into motion and completed the two-block trek down the beach to the Buckmans' high-walled compound.

After soaking in the whirlpool tub and then showering, he donned a terry robe, rewrapped his ankle and foot with the soft cast he'd removed before bathing, and helped himself to a bottle of imported beer from the bar in his suite. He made his way to the spare bedroom that doubled as his temporary office, determined to shift his attention to something other than the woman he'd just met. Despite the editing he needed to do on the raw footage of his most recent documentary, Michael couldn't stop thinking about Elizabeth Parker. He wanted her with a hunger so intense that it unnerved him.

He abandoned the pretense of work within a few minutes of entering his makeshift office. He even considered going to bed, but he felt too restless to sleep. He settled, instead, into a lounge chair on the moon-washed upper patio, setting aside his crutches and indulging himself in what he suspected had the potential of turning into a full-fledged fascination.

Eyes closed and body tense with desire, he felt the cool ocean breeze wash over him. The heat raging through his bloodstream refused to abate, however. If anything, it intensified as evocative images of Elizabeth Parker filled his mind and stimulated his senses. He exhaled raggedly.

He couldn't dismiss her from his mind, so he stopped trying. He reflected on the woman he'd just met, aware that she was a classic study in contrasts. Independent but cautious. Alert but guarded. Self-contained but also outspoken. He'd felt her warming to him while they'd conversed, but his bluntness had upset the tenuous balance between them.

Michael Cassidy prided himself on noticing details—the little things other people invariably missed. It was a quality that had always aided him in his work as a director. It was a quality that haunted him now.

Elizabeth Parker. A woman with a sultry voice that sent his imagination on speculative journeys that were both far-reaching and exotic.

Elizabeth Parker. A woman whose laughter was so incredibly erotic and enticing that it made a joke of the logic he invariably applied to past or prospective liaisons with women.

Elizabeth Parker. A contemporary woman with a centerfold kind of body that invited a man's hungry gaze and made him covet every curve and hollow for himself.

Elizabeth Parker. Poised. Graceful. Not a deliberate seductress or a raving beauty by any means, but an imminently watchable woman nonetheless. A confident woman as well, her fair complexion free of cosmetics, her thick black hair wet and carelessly scraped away from her heart-shaped face, the dense dark lashes framing her eyes spiked with seawater.

He remembered staring at her in those first moments. And he recalled the shock of utterly elemental recognition, abject hunger, and so many other emotions flooding his consciousness that he'd felt momentarily overwhelmed. It hadn't mattered that staring was rude. He hadn't been able to help himself. He took consolation in the fact that she'd studied him with equal intensity, although he knew her motive had been one of self-protection.

Michael couldn't think of a single reason to fault her cautious demeanor, so he didn't, but he continued to marvel over the physical and psychological transformation that had taken place in her the second she'd caught sight of him. Gaze narrowed, head slightly cocked, arms at her sides, and legs apart, she'd been prepared to flee in the space of a heartbeat. That kind of intense awareness in other people floored him, because it was so rare. He'd remarked on it, inadvertently making her even more wary. She'd handled the situation well though, regaining her emotional balance with an ease he still admired.

Elizabeth Parker. Her own person, he realized with satisfaction. The daughter and sister of cops, which explained her heightened awareness of everything around her, not just her obvious absence of fear. She'd been watchful but not afraid. Definitely not afraid.

He thought again about her voice. Low, throaty, and as sensorily erotic as raw silk grazing the skin. His body tautened even more in reaction to his recollection of the sound. He groaned, then swore angrily. He felt needy, and he hated that feeling because it reminded him of the times in his life when no one had responded to his need. It reminded him, as well, of the addictive relationship—they'd called it love—that had existed between his mother and father, the kind of relationship he never intended to experience firsthand with any woman.

He categorically refused to need anyone, even Elizabeth Parker, despite her allure. He remained on the patio, his thoughts drifting at times, but invariably returning to the woman who had shared her laughter and compassion with him for a short while the previous evening. Michael wondered several times that night if she had a man in her life, but he still didn't know the answer as the dawn edged into the sky several hours later.

Michael made his way to the Torrey Pines cliffs on his crutches the following evening, but he moved at a far less reckless pace than the previous night. Filtered light from the homes, restaurants, and the two public parking lots that fronted the beach illuminated his path on the hard-packed sand as the dusk claimed the coastline. Once he completed his exercise regimen, he made himself comfortable on one of the benches at the edge of Seagrove Park—a location that provided a convenient view of the beach.

Michael didn't kid himself about his motives as he sat there. He wanted to see Elizabeth Parker again, although he promised himself that he would leave the outcome of any encounter up to her. If she paused, he intended to greet her. If she ignored him, he would respect her privacy.

She jogged into sight a short while later, clad in a tank-style pale gray unitard that emphasized the shape of her figure, a pair of high-tech-looking athletic shoes favored by long distance runners, and an electric-pink sweatband that held her thick shoulder-length hair off her face. Her pace slowed when she spotted him, and he held his breath until the air in his lungs burned for release.

Michael watched her hesitate. Hope flared within him like the bright light from a beacon. She altered her course, veering across the beach. She smiled as she approached him, and he thought of the first rays of sunshine at the start of a new day as he dealt with the shock and relief he felt.

Winded and damp with perspiration, Elizabeth jogged in a wide circle in front of him. She gradually slowed her pace, her discipline and training evident because she didn't rush the process of allowing her pulse rate to return to normal while her body cooled down. Michael didn't rush her either. He gave her the time she needed to regain her equilibrium, all the while cautioning himself not to say or do anything that would cause her to flee.

"How many miles have you done?" he eventually asked.

"Just under six." Her respiration still faintly uneven, she parked her hands on her hips as she downshifted from a jog to a walk.

"In addition to your evening swim?"

She shook her head. "Instead of. A friend warned me that the undertow played havoc with a lot of swimmers earlier this afternoon." As she spoke, Elizabeth used her terry sweatband to wipe the perspiration from her face and neck, then looped it around her wrist.

"I'm jealous," he admitted.

"Don't be." Her walk tapered off to a stroll. "Before you know it, you'll be back to normal."

"I'm counting on it."

She approached the unoccupied end of the bench a few moments later and propped the heel of one foot on it. Michael watched her bend at the waist and curl her fingers over the toe of her shoe. She rested her forehead on her knee and stretched the muscles in her leg, then repeated the process on the other leg.

He didn't try to hide his appreciation of the toned condition of her body as his gaze traveled over her lithe form, his attention lingering on the more pronounced curves displayed by the form-fitting unitard. Her body was the stuff of erotic male fantasies. He noted, as well, her relaxed demeanor. Although he wondered about the cause, he didn't question his good fortune. His instincts assured him that there'd be time enough later to analyze it. "I think I owe you an apology," he said.

Startled, Elizabeth paused in her stretching and peered at him. "Whatever for?"

"I was hard on you last night."

Not missing a beat, she teased, "Which time?"

Michael grabbed his chest. "I'm mortally wounded, Ms. Parker."

Her grin reappeared, the brilliance of it blinding him once again. "I couldn't resist," she confessed.

"See that you do in the future," he cautioned before he chuckled.

She laughed with him. The sound seduced every single one of his senses all over again. He fell silent for several moments, grappling with the impact she had on him and savoring the view as she resumed her stretching. He no longer felt like the jaded creature his last lover had accused him of being. What he still felt—and it astounded him—was an inexplicable hunger for a woman he barely knew.

Who was she? he wondered in sudden frustration. Why did she inspire cravings within him that he'd long ago convinced himself were far beyond his reach? Suddenly angry with himself, Michael slammed the brakes on his thoughts. He never allowed himself to think this way, never allowed himself to want the closeness that he knew others took for granted, and he didn't intend to start now. Such thoughts reminded him of the past, a past cluttered with broken promises and disillusionment at an early age. He considered that part of his life a closed chapter. He refused to revisit it, because he knew from experience that trips down memory lane were for fools and dreamers. No one had ever accused him of being either, and no one ever would.

"Your laughter kept me awake last night," he announced, shocked by his admission even as the words left his mouth.

Elizabeth grinned. "Oh, dear. I gave the man nightmares."

"Hardly." He thought about the fantasies that had invaded his mind, erotic, torturous fantasies that had made sleep a futile endeavor. Sounding more serious than he meant to, he remarked, "I'm glad to know you're real."

Elizabeth looked startled. "You had some doubt about that?"

"I thought I'd imagined you."

The smile left her face. Straightening slowly, she pinned him with a serious look. "I'm very real, with all the requisite flaws of any human being. Don't ever think otherwise."

"I promise to take your warning to heart."

Elizabeth advised, "You should. Presumptions about people can cause a lot of problems. So can unrealistic expectations."

He recognized the boundary lines she'd just drawn for what they were. Bold enough, though, to take calculated risks, Michael cut to the bottom line. "Does this mean we're going to be friends?" He waited while she pondered his question.

"It means we're finding out if we want to be friends," she said cautiously.

"I want to know you." *Do you, really?* a voice in his head asked. *Don't you just want to sleep with her and then walk away?* He ignored the voice and the questions, and watched her silently debate his sincerity and her potential response as she searched his features in the fading light.

"And I'd like to know you too," she said, but almost too softly to be heard. She looked away, her gaze shifting to the darkness engulfing the coastline.

Michael wondered about her thoughts, but he didn't pry, because he glimpsed what could be described only as vulnerability in her profile. He felt the overwhelming urge to hold her then, to comfort her, as though in doing so he could convey that she had nothing to fear from him. "You're a surprise. I didn't expect to meet someone like you."

"Someone like me?" she said, echoing his statement as she refocused on him.

"Someone I'd want to know."

"You sound very . . . selective."

"Extremely. My friend list is short, but everyone on it is of the long-standing variety."

"I meant it last night when I said that friendship was possible."

"But you seemed to regret your words," Michael reminded her. "You pulled back before you said good night."

She sighed, the sound weighted with an array of emotions. "I was a little impulsive last night, and I was uncertain about your motives. I'm still not certain of them."

Her honesty startled him. He felt compelled to reassure her because the alternative was not something he was willing to risk. He wondered then why she seemed so unaware of her appeal. He also wondered if the men she knew made it a practice to overlook her. Although he doubted his ability to pretend that he didn't desire her, he decided to try. At least for then.

"What are you thinking?" she asked.

"I'm thinking that I'll try not to ask anything of you that you can't give. You make the rules, Elizabeth Parker, and I'll do my damnedest to abide by them."

Her shock was evident. "You're serious, aren't you?"

"Very serious."

She didn't speak for a moment. He sensed she was wrestling with a variety of issues, not simply his willingness to meet her terms. He discovered within himself a desire to understand all the issues that drove her, especially the ones that made her hesitate or made her accessible.

"I'm going to hold you to your promise," she said.

Michael nodded. "I expect you to."

"How are you feeling?" she asked, changing the subject without warning.

He chuckled, the sound reminiscent of rustling October leaves. "Like a chicken."

Confused, she just looked at him.

A smile flirted with his mouth. "Cooped up."

Her eyes twinkled with sudden humor. "Have you seen your doctor?"

"Earlier today, as a matter of fact."

"And . . . ?" she encouraged.

"And as of next Monday I graduate to daily physical therapy. And at least two more weeks on the crutches. After that I can get around on my own, but no marathons for at least another six months."

"That's very good news."

Michael nodded, but caution remained etched into the lines of his angular features. "There's an end in sight."

"Think of it as a new beginning," she suggested.

He looked skeptical. "If you say so."

She smiled. "I'm what's known as an optimist."

"But not naive."

Her smile immediately disappeared. "No, not naive."

"I hear regret in your voice. Why?"

"It's hard to explain," she hedged.

He decided that whatever she was hiding was both painful and important. "Will you try once you're more comfortable with me?"

"I honestly don't know if I can. Explain, I mean. What happens once you're off the crutches?"

He let her change the subject, although he promised himself that he would find the key to her secrets. He refused to dwell on why he wanted access to every facet of her life and personality. "I get my life back."

She sank down onto the bench, drew her legs up,

and looped her arms around them. Resting her chin on her knees, she studied him with a thoughtful expression. The evening breeze tugged at the curling tendrils of dark hair that framed her face. "And what kind of a life do you have, Michael Cassidy?"

"A very good one," he said, feeling a surge of pride in what he'd created for himself in the eighteen years since he'd graduated from film school in Los Angeles.

"Where do you live this good life?"

"I have a place in L.A."

"A house or a condo?"

He smiled, because even his close friends had a hard time with his willingness to live and work in an industrial complex. "Not exactly a house. More like a large building that happens to have a loft that I use for living quarters. Industrial motif, I guess you'd call it."

"Sounds unusual."

"It probably is, now that I think about it, but space is important to me."

"Are you claustrophobic?"

"On some levels I probably am," he conceded with a shrug, suddenly feeling uncomfortable. The shabby two-room apartment of his youth came into view in his mind. It wasn't a time or a place that he liked to remember. In particular, he hated remembering the rejection and isolation of those years, but he was an honest man, honest enough to realize that his childhood had influenced many of his adult choices. "I like a lot of space when I'm working."

"And do you like your work?"

"I can't imagine doing anything else."

She looked at him expectantly. "What is it that you do?" she asked.

He thought she was kidding, until he really looked at her. Her expressive facial features, especially her large, dark eyes, made him realize that she wasn't being coy. She honestly didn't know, which was momentarily humbling for a man accustomed to being pursued by all manner of people because of his professional credentials. He suddenly liked the fact that she wasn't a star chaser. There were a sufficient number of those types in Hollywood, and he loathed dodging them.

"I record life on the streets," he told her, purposefully vague.

"You've given me a puzzle to solve," she mused.

He smiled then. "Need another clue?"

She held up her hand, clearly willing to accept his challenge without further assistance. "You're in the film business."

"That was easy. At least half the people in Del Mar are a part of the business."

She nodded. "It was kind of obvious, since you know the Buckmans, and Hal's got a reputation here at the beach as one of the movers and shakers in Hollyweird."

Michael winced. "Hollyweird?"

She grinned. Her expression contained such childish glee that he didn't have the heart to take her to task over the slur.

"Sure you don't want another clue?"

"Nope." Elizabeth studied him. She even stood and made a show of walking around and inspecting him from a variety of angles. "Please tell me that you don't do disease-of-the-week or psychological-trauma-of-the-month movies for network television."

He managed not to laugh out loud. "And if I did?"

"I'd very politely wish you additional professional success in the future."

His smile faded as he watched her worry her bottom lip with her teeth. Her gaze grew speculative, the tip of her tongue darting out to bathe the area that she'd temporarily dented with her teeth. Michael smothered the groan the tantalizing sight provoked. He could almost feel her mouth, her lips, the stroking of her tongue on his skin. He wanted a taste of her. He longed to touch her. Everywhere. He craved the feel of her curves pressed against his body. He wanted so much from her, but he knew better than to let himself want a woman like Elizabeth Parker. He'd already recognized her for what she was—a forever kind of woman, and that kind was dangerous for a man like him. He'd seen firsthand the destructive power of love gone wrong and trust misplaced. His parents had paid the price for their poor judgment and immaturity. Thanks to the love-hate relationship they'd shared, he'd been left in their marital rubble with the task of reconstructing his childhood.

Despite his melancholy thoughts, his body became aroused as his desire for her spiked. Michael shifted on the bench, trying to ease his physical discomfort. Clearing his throat, he remarked in what he hoped was a normal-sounding voice, "Methinks the lady is stumped."

"You don't run one of the networks, do you?"

Wincing, he didn't even try to conceal his distaste. "Not my style at all."

"You value your independence," she mused. "You dislike taking orders from other people. You're essentially a loner, but you've managed to turn that characteristic into an asset in your career. How am I doing so far?"

"Extremely accurate. I'm feeling quite transparent just about now."

"You're an independent filmmaker," she guessed. "Your subject matter runs the gamut, but my instincts tell me that you prefer dealing with realistic topics, perhaps even relevant social issues."

"I'm impressed. I direct documentary films, but I do them only on a project-by-project basis for the major studios."

"You're a control freak."

"Probably," he said without any remorse.

"And proud of it," she noted, her amusement obvious.

He grinned, suddenly not minding the transparency of his personality where this woman was concerned. "Totally."

"Are you always so unrepentant?"

He laughed, delighted by her directness. "Always."

"You must give people fits."

"Some of the men and women who work for me have wisely invested in a company that makes antacids."

"Oh, dear. Attila the Hun reincarnated."

"Does this mean you don't want my autograph?"

"Maybe next year."

"Only if I win another Oscar?"

"Braggart," she accused, laughter lighting her thickly lashed dark eyes.

"You're not impressed?"

She pursed her lips, then nodded. "Of course I'm impressed, but only by the size of your ego."

"You wound me."

"Shall I call a doctor?"

"I really have to win another Oscar for you to be interested in my signature?"

"Absolutely."

"Although I think that's very superficial of you, I'll make it my goal."

"What type of films do you make?" she asked, her tone turning serious.

"The type that make people very uncomfortable, if the reviewers are to be believed."

"Specifically?" she pressed.

"Reality-based films about inner-city living."

"With a unique theme for each one? Like unemployment, drugs, gang violence, health issues, that sort of thing?"

He nodded, glad she understood. Her agile mind and native curiosity showed. He looked for those qualities in the people he welcomed into his life. Michael amended his last thought to *when* he welcomed someone into his life. He rarely did, he realized. He felt less vulnerable that way.

"Michael?"

He flashed her a quick smile, willing to be distracted from the path his mind seemed inclined to travel. "That's my name."

"Should I know your work?"

"You probably do, whether or not you realize it. Some of what I've done has shown up on various television networks in the U.S. and Europe for rebroadcast during the last ten years or so."

"It's definitely not entertainment, is it?"

"Only if your perspective of the world is totally skewed."

Michael realized that his comment had triggered something unsettling within her. He saw the change in her the instant it began—an almost complete retreat into a private place that was exclusively hers. Once again he realized that something weighed very heavily on her.

"Are you chilled?" he asked, his concern increasing when a shudder ran through her.

Elizabeth shook her head as she met his gaze. "Not really."

"Problem?" he asked.

She looked genuinely startled by his question, so startled, in fact, that he couldn't help wondering yet again about the people in her life. Hadn't they noticed that something was eating at her? Didn't they care enough to try to help her through whatever it was?

"No, no problem," she hastily assured him. "It's too nice a night to be troubled."

"Someday, when we've known each other longer, I won't let you dodge my questions," he cautioned.

"Perhaps I won't want to dodge them," she said with her usual candor.

"I hope not."

"Tell me more about your work. Is that how you met Hal Buckman?"

"He was my mentor when I first got into the business. We've worked on several projects together over the years."

"He's a gruff old guy, isn't he?"

Michael smiled in response to her good manners. Most people he knew cursed when expressing themselves on the subject of Hal Buckman. "Bull's-eye. Heart of gold though, as clichéd as that probably sounds."

"His kids never seemed to mind the way he growled at everyone."

"Diane," he said, referring to Hal's wife of forty years, "contends that he's a pussycat under all that bluff and bluster."

"Is he as powerful as people say?"

He nodded. "Probably more so."

"He never throws his weight around when he's here. I've always liked that about him. Some of our part-time residents, especially the ones who seem to need the constant stroking of their fans and the media, are remarkably self-absorbed," Elizabeth said.

Michael didn't mount a defense of the less-secure personalities in the film industry. Although tactfully stated, he knew that Elizabeth's observations were accurate. As he thought about Hal Buckman, Michael wondered who else would have taken the time to mentor a scrappy kid who'd grown up on the streets, a smart-mouthed twenty-year-old who'd had a sky-scraper-size chip on his shoulder? He doubted that anyone but Hal, who had grown up on those same mean streets, would have had the patience to cope with his defensiveness while successfully nurturing his talent.

"Are you originally from San Diego?" he asked in an effort to shift the conversation back to Elizabeth.

She nodded. "I'm a native."

He chuckled, recalling her affinity with the sea. "Of the Pacific or California?"

"Both, actually." Grinning, she confessed, "I love the ocean. It's where I feel the most secure."

He studied her, amazed by her revealing remark. He silently speculated that Elizabeth Parker had apparently failed to find emotional safety in her relationships, and he wondered why. He didn't bother to ask himself the same question, because he already knew the answer. He trusted no one with his emotions. "You aren't kidding, are you?"

"Of course not. I understand the unpredictable nature of the ocean, and I respect it. In an odd way, I think it respects me."

"Interesting perspective."

"Not one you've ever heard before?" she asked.

"Precisely." Michael shrugged. "But then, I don't spend much time at the beach."

"But now that you're here . . ." she began to say.

Her smile engaged his senses so thoroughly that he longed to pull her into his arms and kiss her, but he managed to control himself. "Now that I'm here," he said, filling in the space she'd provided as his gaze swept over her. He made no effort to conceal his appreciation. "I've discovered that the beach is a very appealing place. In fact, it's far more appealing than I'd ever imagined."

Her smile slipped. Michael watched it become achingly tentative as she peered at him. His gut told him that her self-confidence had taken a recent beating. He wondered how and why, and by whom, but he kept his curiosity to himself. He silently vowed, though, that he would find a way to understand the glimpses of vulnerability she unwittingly provided.

Seated on the bench in the semidarkness, they chatted easily until the last evening train from Los Angeles arrived nearly an hour later at the Amtrak station located across the street from the beachfront park. Elizabeth glanced at the luminous dial of her wristwatch.

"Time to go?" Michael asked.

"Past time, unfortunately," she answered, although she didn't explain why.

He reached for his crutches. She stood, her gaze on him as he got up and hooked the crutches under his arms. He moved toward her, his expression intent. The expectant look on her face inspired intimacy. Rocked once again by desire for her, he tightened his grip on his crutches, willing himself not to get any closer to her, willing himself not to place his hands on her because he knew he wouldn't be able to let go.

"What's wrong?" she whispered, confusion flickering in her eyes.

He shook his head. "Nothing's wrong. I was just thinking about how much I like you, Elizabeth Parker."

Her smile reappeared. "Ditto, Michael Cassidy," she said softly, using his word of the previous night.

"I'll walk you home."

Elizabeth nodded. "I'd like that."

As they had the night before, they ended their time together near the retaining wall that circled the beach side of her property. They wished each other well, but said nothing about future meetings.

Michael spent yet another restless night at the Buckman compound.

THREE

Elizabeth stopped questioning the instincts that guided her to Michael each evening following their first two encounters at the edge of the Pacific. It hadn't taken her long to realize that she trusted him in ways that she hadn't trusted another person in a very long time. He was a surprise she hadn't expected, but also a temptation unlike any she'd experienced.

She refrained from mentioning his presence in her life to anyone. Michael was her secret, her reward at the end of the daily sessions devoted to her studies at the university library. Unlike her family and friends, he knew only what she felt inclined to reveal about herself. And unlike her family and friends, he could neither judge nor decry the choices she'd made. Elizabeth appreciated having a clean slate. It freed her, if only temporarily, from being linked to the tragedy that had taken place the previous year. She intended to share the truth with him at the right moment, but she welcomed this reprieve from the nightmare that had turned her life upside down.

She enjoyed their conversations, which were punctuated by laughter and jumped around from abstract political theory to sand-blasting as an art form to the current status of the NASA space program.

The hours they shared lengthened with each successive evening they spent together. As they grew closer she learned of the high premium Michael placed on integrity and personal honor, primarily because he kept his promise to respect the boundary lines she'd drawn during their first meeting. She also valued those character traits, despite the nagging sense of unease she felt over what he would think of her when he eventually learned the truth. Estranged from her family and deeply disillusioned by her fiancé's lack of support, she still struggled with the self-doubt their collective disapproval had generated.

Elizabeth didn't pretend that Michael wasn't attracted to her. Neither did she pretend that she wasn't drawn to him. He filled a hollow place in her heart, a place that had been, until then, littered with nothing more than the echoes of isolation and loneliness. Mature enough to recognize the signs of their mutual attraction and honest enough with herself to confront them, she suspected that his promise not to breach those invisible boundary lines she'd established was all that kept him from acknowledging or acting on the chemistry flowing between them—the pulse-pounding, heart-racing, hunger-rooted-deep-in-the-soul kind of chemistry that makes a man and woman desire each other in the most elemental of ways.

At first she told herself that she'd simply fallen in lust with a virile man, but her heart assured her that what she felt for him contained the potential of becoming more vital and far more emotionally encompassing than anything she'd ever before experienced in a relationship with a man. For a while she even hoped that her feelings for Michael would abate with the passage of time, but they didn't. Instead, her emotions intensified with every passing hour. Determined not to complicate their relationship, yet torn between appreciating Michael's integrity and wishing that he would simply respond to the desire arcing like an electrical current between them, she walked an emotional tightrope whenever they were together. She feared the inevitable fall as well as the crippling aftermath.

Several days following their initial meeting, Elizabeth completed her nightly swim a few minutes before the sun slipped beyond the edge of the horizon. She spotted Michael as she found her footing in the swirling surf. Waving at him, she made her way across the beach to the park. Once there, she hurriedly dried herself with the towel he handed her and then donned the oversize cherry-red sweatshirt she'd left on the bench before going into the water.

"How was your swim?" Michael asked as she sat down beside him.

She finger-combed her hair off her forehead and away from her cheeks. Her eyes sparkled, a smile playing at the corners of her mouth as she spoke. "Just what I needed."

"I'm looking forward to joining you one of these nights. I've always wanted to go swimming with a woman who's part sea otter."

She grinned at him, not at all offended by the comparison. He already knew, thanks to her description of the volunteer work she'd done with the Wildlife Foundation, that she had a soft spot in her heart for the sleek creatures of the sea.

Her gaze drifted over him, her thoughts fleeing and her awareness of everything around them fading. Elizabeth felt her senses come alive as she took in the muscular power of his body. The desire she experienced just looking at him made her insides throb and her heart ache for shared intimacy.

As if sensing her distraction, he frowned. "Penny for your thoughts."

He spoke so softly that she felt as though he'd whispered the words along the side of her neck. She trembled, searching his expressive features in the dim light and wondering if he felt the tug she felt, hungered as she did for something more tangible between them. "I doubt they're worth that much," she finally confessed, knowing that even as she spoke, she lied. She hadn't felt so alive in years.

He reached out, startling her when he smoothed his callused fingertips over her knuckles. Elizabeth stared at him, the air in her lungs trapped when she inhaled sharply. She didn't pull away. She savored the physical connection. It wasn't the first time Michael had deliberately touched her. He often handed her a towel after a swim, and the casual brush of his fingertips invariably sent her senses spinning out of control. She felt her heart thrum with anticipation as she looked at him.

She deliberately turned her wrist, their palms meeting and mating on contact. His hand, so much larger, so much more powerful, encompassed hers. She felt his strength, not just his body's warmth, as he wove their fingers together. The heat of his skin reminded her of a brand, a brand that had the power to reach her soul. She exhaled shakily, her emotions in disarray.

"Tough day?" he asked, his voice rougher-sounding than usual, his fingers tightening possessively around hers, his gaze so hot, her senses sizzled.

"Not really. Just long."

"Want to talk about it?"

Elizabeth shrugged. "There's not that much to tell. I started at the library when it opened at seven."

"Why so early?"

"I'm scheduled to be a teaching assistant when the semester starts in September, plus I've begun the research for my thesis. Lots to do."

"Why psychology?" he asked, already aware of her major thanks to a previous conversation.

She told him the unvarnished truth. "I want a better understanding of what motivates people." She paused, emotion rising up in her and almost swamping her self-control. "I really need to understand why people do the things they do."

Michael frowned, looking for all the world like a

man with a new puzzle to assemble. "Interesting choice," he remarked.

"I want to go into adult counseling once I finish my master's program." She didn't mention that she eventually hoped to specialize in crisis intervention, because such a revelation would invite questions she wasn't ready to answer.

"A worthy endeavor," Michael said in the same neutral tone. "But there's something troubling you, and I don't think it has anything to do with the day you've just had or your course load."

His challenge was clear. Even though he was right on target, she didn't want to admit that she felt edgy because she couldn't get her feelings for him under control, or that she was still hauling around unresolved baggage from her past. She deliberately hedged. "I'm just tired, Michael."

He exhaled. Elizabeth heard the disappointment in the sound. She felt guilty, but not guilty enough to offer a truth-filled confession.

"I want to hold you."

She stared at him, thoroughly startled and wondering if she'd heard him correctly. She also wondered exactly when she'd become so transparent in her desire for him that he'd discovered her secret.

"Why?" she asked, then promptly regretted even opening her mouth.

"Do I need a reason?" he asked quietly.

"No," she whispered.

"Would you prefer it if I didn't touch you?"

She consciously gave up the battle for rational behavior, surrendering to her feelings as she moved toward him. "I want you to hold me."

"Elizabeth . . ." He groaned.

She paused, searching his features. "Did I say something wrong?"

"Not wrong. Never wrong. I guess it was my turn to be surprised."

Still feeling off balance, she managed a faint smile. The past tugged at her while fledgling hope for a happier future, not just her desire for this man, seduced her. "Shall I apologize?"

He chuckled. Taking her hands, he drew her closer. They studied each other, both seeking answers to questions as yet unasked.

"No apology necessary," he said. "I don't mind being surprised. I also didn't mean to push you. You're still in charge, so we're not going anywhere or doing anything you don't want to do." He paused, as though to weigh the wisdom of what he was about to say. "It's just that I've wondered since that first night what it would be like to hold you in my arms. I need to know, Elizabeth. I really need to know."

Mesmerized by the raw sound of his voice, she nodded. "I understand, because I need to know too."

She felt the tremor her admission sent through his body. He released her hands and opened his arms to her, allowing her to choose the contact she found most acceptable. Elizabeth quelled her initial impulse, which was to throw caution to the wind and hurl herself directly at him. Too much was at stake for her to be guilty of thoughtless behavior. Turning so that her back was to him, she leaned against his chest and rested her head on his shoulder.

She didn't resist when he brought his arms around her and criss-crossed them beneath her breasts. Inhaling the citrusy scent of his cologne, she basked in his strength and in the utter sense of rightness she felt in Michael's embrace. A buoy clanged in the distance, and the running lights of a tanker marked the distant night-engulfed horizon. She sighed, the sound a reflection of the diverse emotions coursing through her.

"Thank you," Elizabeth said, feeling so much that she nearly wept.

"For what?"

"Lots of things."

His arms brushed the undersides of her breasts. Elizabeth felt her nipples tighten into hard points of sensation. She trembled when an image of his hands skimming over her naked body slipped into her mind.

"You're very welcome," he said.

She forced herself beyond the tantalizing images streaming like an erotic film through her head and the hunger she felt, although her voice shook as she spoke. "I rented one of your documentaries from the local video store this afternoon."

"Which one?"

"*Inner City Gangs.*"

He chuckled. "Now I understand your mood."

She didn't contradict him. Her mood had absolutely nothing to do with a video. It had everything to do with this man and what she wanted to share with him. "You took some very real risks when you shot that film."

"No more than anyone else involved in the production."

Elizabeth didn't believe him. She'd sensed from the beginning that he was a bona fide risk taker. She also doubted that he was anything but obsessive about his own professional agenda. Since she knew the inner-city streets far better than he would have ever guessed, she realized what he'd been up against, but she opted not to argue with him.

"I liked the balance you achieved in the perspectives of the gang members, their leaders, and the police. I was also impressed by the humanity of the project. Your work is very powerful. You obviously deserve the awards you've received."

"Thank you, but what's really powerful is how much I want you," he muttered through gritted teeth.

She closed her eyes for a moment, breathing shallowly and wondering how to cope with such a comment. Honesty, she decided, was a double-edged sword. "Michael . . ." she began to say.

"Holding back isn't something I do well," he confessed, his head bowed and his breath bathing her cheek with moist heat as he spoke. He nuzzled the side of her neck with his lips, sending glittering sensations on a journey across her skin. Her insides clenched in response, and the ache deep inside her simply grew more encompassing.

"You've done remarkably well so far," she softly reminded him.

"All I ever seem to think about is holding you and

touching you and tasting you. I'm not *doing* worth a damn."

She turned in his arms. She felt his hands lock in place at her waist. Reaching up, she cupped his face between her palms. Her fingertips rested atop the pulse beating in his temple as she studied his strained expression. Her skin tingled in response to the beard stubble covering his jaw. Elizabeth absently decided that he hadn't taken the time to shave that morning. It gave him a reckless look, a look that matched his personality. "I'm curious too."

He covered one of her hands with his own and guided it to his mouth. Pressing a kiss into the center of her open palm, he then moved on to the pulse pounding at her wrist. He kept his eyes on her the entire time, and Elizabeth's heart quivered in response to the hunger she saw in his gaze. It was a mirror reflection of the hunger she felt for him.

"I want a taste of you as well." The words spilled past her lips before she could stop them, shocking her.

He paused, restraint tautening his body. "But . . . ?"

She stared at him, utterly captivated by the promise of passion visible in his face and eyes. The caution and common sense intrinsic to her personality surfaced. "I'm certain that one taste wouldn't be enough. I'd want much more, Michael."

He exhaled raggedly. "You never cease to amaze me."

"Why?"

"You don't play word games. You're the most honest woman I've ever met."

Elizabeth's heart almost stopped beating. She'd heard several variations of that comment from a variety of people all her life. Do you always have to be so damn honest! The last time she'd endured the words, they'd been in the form of an accusation thrown at her by her former fiancé. She squared her shoulders, failing to keep the defensiveness she felt under wraps. "You were warned."

Gathering her stiff form into his arms, Michael brought her into his heat. His body reminded her of a furnace. He held her close, but he didn't trap her. She sensed that he would free her the instant she pulled back, so she didn't struggle.

"I'm not complaining."

"And I'm not apologizing, Michael."

"Don't apologize," he urged. "And don't ever change."

She smiled, relaxing against his chest once she heard his sincerity. Elizabeth felt the leashed strength of his muscular body as her breasts plumped against the hard wall above his heart. She slid her hands around his neck, instinct guiding her as she tangled her fingers at his nape and rested her cheek on his shoulder. She absorbed the shudder that moved through his large frame, but she didn't say anything. She simply let herself feel the emotional intimacy they shared, all the while wondering about Michael's ability as a lover. She suspected that the patience and restraint he exercised now spoke volumes about his skill, but she wanted and needed more from him than skill. Much, much more.

"You're killing me, woman," he muttered a few minutes later.

She looked up at him at the same instant he looked down at her. Time stuttered to a stop. They were both tantalized by the desire they felt, both waiting, both breathlessly aware that there were tough decisions ahead.

He swore, then dragged enough air into his body to fill his lungs. "Talk to me, Elizabeth. Tell me about your family."

She blinked in surprise at the desperation she heard in his voice. He desired her even more than she'd initially realized, and that knowledge made her heart soar. "What would you like to know?"

"Anything. Everything. Just talk to me."

She eased backward, trying to lessen the temptation caused by the intimate alignment of their bodies, but she didn't shift beyond the circle of his loose embrace. "Talking about my family's not always that easy."

"I am," he groused.

Grateful that he hadn't registered her reticence on the subject of her family, and far too hungry for him to pretend otherwise, she exhaled shakily. "You're advertising," she chided.

He chuckled, the sound utterly ragged. "I'm serious, you know."

She pursed her lips, then intoned, "Obsessive-compulsive personality tendencies. Patient also excessively self-absorbed."

"Real nice, Ms. Parker. I think you've dented my psyche and my ego."

Elizabeth grinned, then promptly shifted gears for both their sakes. They were in a public place, and groping each other like teenagers in a parked car wasn't something she wanted to indulge in, no matter how much she desired him. She opted for the safety of memories that didn't hurt. "My parents were childhood sweethearts."

He looked baffled. "Excuse me?"

"You asked about my family," she pointed out. "I thought I'd start at the beginning."

"I did, didn't I? By all means, start at the beginning."

"They're originally from Chicago, but they visited California on their honeymoon and decided to stay."

"Impulsive people. I like that." He gave her a curious look. "What happened to you?"

She smiled and shrugged, not minding his question. She'd heard it before, although in a different context. Michael, she knew, was simply teasing her. "I guess they ran out of impulsive genes before they had me."

"You're the baby of your family?"

She winced. "I have that dubious honor, and no one ever lets me forget it. My judgment is constantly maligned." The truth she spoke wounded her heart even before she uttered the words. Why, she wondered for the thousandth time, hadn't they been there for her when she'd needed them the most? Her family's shame had been apparent when she'd resigned from the force, and it still colored her self-image and a relationship she'd once believed she would always be able to rely upon.

"You mentioned brothers."

"I did, didn't I?"

He nodded. As they sat on the bench, he held her hand and traced invisible designs in her palm. She watched some of his tension slowly fade from his features. She felt some of her own depart as well.

"Two brothers," she confirmed. "Both are married, both have children, and both are in law enforcement. Tom's a deputy sheriff, and Mark's a motorcycle officer with the local police department. I also have an older sister. Gabriella is a pediatrician."

"And your dad?"

"Retired now, but he was the chief of police in a neighboring community for several years. He and Mom spend most of their time in their RV these days. I think Dad's trying to make up for all those years when work was his first priority. They're in Alaska this summer."

"I'm surprised you didn't go into law enforcement too."

"My entire family thought it was a lousy idea," she said honestly.

Michael slid his arm around her shoulders and drew her close. "I'm glad you listened to them. The thought of you standing in the line of fire on a daily basis isn't real appealing."

But I didn't listen, she thought as she rested her head against his shoulder and stared at the star-cluttered night sky, *and the price was incredibly high*.

"I want to make love to you," he said.

Stunned, Elizabeth went absolutely still inside.

"Does it bother you that I want you so much?"

"No," she whispered.

When she said nothing more, he asked, "What are you thinking?"

"That I want you just as much, even though I'm not ready to take that step." She lifted her head from his shoulder and looked at him. "I don't know when I will be."

"I'll wait," he ground out. "I'm willing to wait as long as it takes."

Elizabeth spoke softly. "I think I've known that since the beginning."

And she did know that about him, she realized. Michael cared enough about her to be patient, and she valued that quality in him. He was a strong man, a man of his word. A real man, like her father and her brothers. But would he judge her as harshly as they had? she wondered. She knew instinctively that her entire family would approve of Michael. What worried her, though, was the wall she sensed that he'd built around his heart.

Would he ever risk his emotions with her, or would he offer her only his passion? Until she knew the answer to those questions, Elizabeth felt compelled to resist the seductive temptation he posed, no matter how difficult the task.

FOUR

Michael absently watched the plump gray clouds that clustered at odd intervals across the amethyst-colored sky. The setting sun straddled the distant horizon like a child perched on a fence rail. Michael's gaze shifted to the white-capped waves that dominated the Pacific while he waited for Elizabeth. She was unlike any woman he'd ever known. Although he savored the hours he shared with the unique woman who never failed to stimulate his imagination and his senses, he realized that she posed an emotional danger—one that he felt helpless to resist even as it drew him deeper and deeper into a labyrinth of feelings and needs that grew more complex each day.

As he sat on their park bench, Michael noted the absence of her towel and sweatshirt, items Elizabeth usually left as a signal to him that she'd gone swimming. He hoped she had decided to run on the beach that evening, because he'd heard the National Weather

Service radio broadcasts urging local swimmers and surfers to use caution if they planned to take on the heavy seas caused by the turbulent weather pattern that had been hopscotching the Pacific for the last eighteen hours. Michael felt confident that she would heed the warning if she heard it.

Closing his eyes, he listened to the waves crashing against the shoreline. He consciously tried to relinquish the tension that had built up inside of him that day. He'd been editing raw film footage for several hours, a tedious but ultimately fulfilling task, and he needed a break.

Clad in a long-sleeved polo shirt he hadn't bothered to tuck in, a pair of faded, age-softened jeans that he'd ripped open at the seam from ankle to calf in order to accommodate his soft cast, and leather thongs, his attire reflected the cooler evening temperatures and gusting breezes caused by the offshore weather disturbance. Michael liked the reckless display put on by Mother Nature. It matched his current mood to a T.

Dusk slowly crept across the sky. Michael lost track of time as he sat there. He didn't even notice Elizabeth's arrival.

"Are we having a picnic?" she asked in that unforgettable voice of hers.

He recognized the sound instantly, hunger exploding inside of him the instant he spotted her. She stood just a few feet away. The diffused glow of a halogen streetlight made it easy for Michael to see the easy smile that lifted the corners of her sensual mouth. The erratic breeze played havoc with her hair and molded the sapphire windsuit she wore to the curves and hollows of her body.

Her clothing, coupled with her subtle use of cosmetics and dry hair, told him that she'd come directly from her cottage. Gazing at her, Michael longed to touch her. He felt his fingertips and palms start to itch with the need, so he closed his hands into fists.

The utter clarity of his next thought caught him off guard. He ached with the craving to possess this woman. He wanted her in his bed, their bodies naked and their limbs entwined. He wanted to sink into her until they became one flesh and then ride out the storm he knew would ensue. He wanted to hear the sensual intonations of her whiskey voice as she moaned her pleasure and whispered his name. And then, each time she neared her summit, he wanted to feel her skin turn to hot silk as she began to unravel in his arms. But most of all, he wanted to lose himself in her and forget the loneliness of his life—a life spent haunted by the failings of the two people whose relationship had destroyed his ability to trust anyone with his emotions. Being around Elizabeth had very nearly persuaded him that she could make him forget the closed-off place that was his heart, if only temporarily.

Michael Cassidy wanted Elizabeth Parker with an intensity that made the desire he'd experienced for the women he had known and bedded before her seem like nothing more than adolescent cravings. The depth of his hunger for her still shook him. That same hunger had been steadily chipping away at the armor that protected his starving heart since their first moments together.

Michael wanted everything that Elizabeth Parker had to give. Everything. But he didn't know quite how to ask for what he wanted. He'd never learned to do anything but take, and he knew in his gut that if he tried to take anything from her, he would lose her. He silently vowed that he would never let that happen.

Michael watched her smile turn into a frown. He felt as though he'd been slapped in the face by reality, and he straightened in response to her obvious confusion. He also remembered where they were, not just his vow to respect the boundary lines she'd drawn during their first moments together. He recalled, as well, an oft-repeated cliché about something being better than nothing. He knew then why he'd always loathed clichés.

"Are we having a picnic, Michael?" She eyed the wedge of Brie, a pull-apart loaf of bread from a local bakery, slices of fresh fruit, and the chocolate-dipped strawberries that had been arranged on a oversize paper plate. Tucked beneath the edge of the plate were bright red napkins, the edges fluttering in the early evening breeze.

Her question penetrated the haze that engulfed him. "We're having whatever the hell we want." He sounded harsh, and he knew it, but instead of apologizing he simply gestured at the vacant end of the bench. "Make yourself comfortable."

She hesitated. "Is your ankle bothering you?"

He shook his head and marshaled his wits. He realized then that Elizabeth had interpreted his silence, and then his frustration, as an indication that he was in pain. He felt like a fool. He was a fool, he concluded. "Of course not."

Looking faintly bemused by his loss of temper, she took a seat on the stone bench.

"This is a lovely surprise. Your timing is perfect."

He enjoyed her appreciation, although it provoked the realization that he rarely took the time to share the simpler pleasures. He allowed very few people into the private part of his life, and he shared himself even less. Michael reached for the backpack at his feet, but his body still throbbed with desire and his bloodstream felt like rivers of flame were rushing through it. His situation would have been laughable if his anatomy hadn't hurt so much.

"Wine or fruit juice?" he asked, anger and need making his voice ragged as he withdrew two small thermoses from the backpack.

"Juice, please."

"No time to jog tonight?" He filled a plastic cup and handed it to her, then poured a few inches of wine into a second cup for himself.

"Between the weather advisories and the day I thought I might end up having, I decided to run this morning. It turned out to be a good decision."

"The library again?" he asked.

Elizabeth nodded after taking a sip of the juice. "And a meeting for all the teaching assistants. The head of the department likes the sound of his own voice, so the meeting went on forever." Reaching for an orange segment, she confessed, "I'm starved. No time for food since breakfast." She popped the slice of orange into her mouth and bit into it. Sinking back against the bench, her eyes fell closed. She groaned, her appreciation for the succulent fruit apparent and tantalizing.

He cursed under his breath. Everything Elizabeth did, every gesture, however innocent, seemed designed lately to make him want her more. She'd be the death of him if he weren't careful.

Although he tried to calm himself, Michael felt his senses go on full alert. His body surged with renewed response to her innate sensuality. He wondered then if she grasped the sensory impact she had on him. Why would she? a rational voice in the back of his mind asked. Elizabeth Cassidy wasn't a mind reader, and he'd never been the kind of man who shared his feelings. Because his past had taught him to guard his emotions, he did so instinctively.

"Your schedule seems to be getting more hectic." His voice still resembled ground glass, thanks to the desire pummeling his insides.

She flashed a grin in his direction as she reached for another orange slice. "Does it count that I'm loving every minute of it?"

He smiled, savoring this unexpected glimpse of the little girl within the sensual woman. "It counts," he said, sensing not for the first time her potential for passionate playfulness. His thoughts sent another tremor of desire through his body, and the wine in the cup he held sloshed over the sides. Disgusted with himself, he reached for a napkin and dried his hand.

Elizabeth declared, "We need a toast."

He waited for her to continue.

"To . . . friendship," she said, her smile achingly vulnerable. "To our friendship."

Although surprised, Michael echoed her words and added some of his own. "To our friendship. May it last for a very long time." As he looked at her, he realized that she'd just unlocked a door to herself that had been sealed until then. She was expressing her trust, formally welcoming him into her life. He refused to question her decision. He needed access to this woman despite the price they'd both end up paying.

They raised their cups at the same time, brought them together for a gentle tap, and then drank in silence. Their eyes met and locked, their eye contact burning with sudden intensity. Awareness arced between them. Elizabeth looked away first, but only a heartbeat before Michael saw something akin to hunger in her gaze. Experience told him it was hunger for *him*, and he felt momentarily triumphant. He also knew he couldn't sustain forever the restraint and abstinence she seemed to need.

"You remind me of myself," he remarked several moments later.

"In what way?" She reached for a napkin as she spoke.

He noted the tremor in her fingers and felt a burst of satisfaction explode within him. "You take your commitments very seriously."

"I always have."

"Most people don't. They just put in their time."

"Then they're not doing what makes them happy."

Michael frowned. Never one to make a secret of his opinions, he remarked, "That is the ultimate cliché." He sounded contemptuous, but he couldn't help himself. He possessed little tolerance for people who lacked the strength of will to properly manage their lives.

"You're being very judgmental, Michael."

"You're right, I am. I have no patience with people who squander time or opportunities. As far as I'm concerned, there won't ever be enough hours in the day for all the things I want to do."

"A typical ambitious Type A," she teased, obviously trying to lighten the moment and his mood. "You, sir, love your work."

"How can you tell?" he asked, amused by the certainty in her voice and her determination to shift the conversation back to him—a tactic she never seemed to tire of.

She arched an elegant brow. "It's impossible to miss. Your passion for what you do brings the documentaries to life."

Michael relaxed. "Thank you, ma'am."

"Not an original observation, I'm sure. After all, the reviewers have already figured you out."

"As much as I resent their criticism at times, I suppose they serve a useful purpose." Michael drained the wine from his cup, set it aside, and slathered Brie on a chunk of bread. "Diane Buckman contends that the only person capable of loving a reviewer is the woman who gave birth to him. I'm inclined to agree with her most of the time."

Elizabeth's delight showed in her laughter. "She's always struck me as a very savvy lady."

"You've been tested big-time, haven't you?" he asked without warning, insight prompting the tough question as he tore the chunk of cheese-topped bread apart and handed her a portion.

Although Elizabeth accepted the bread, she didn't answer his question right away. But that didn't surprise Michael, who felt no remorse for turning the tables on her.

"We're changing the subject already?" she asked.

This evening's match has begun, ladies and gentlemen. "Indulge me."

Looking away, she exhaled softly before she spoke. "Everyone's been tested at one time or another, Michael. I'm no exception."

"I'm not talking about everyone. I'm talking about you."

"I noticed."

He wasn't sure why he felt the need to press her, but he did. "What happened to you was painful. I catch glimpses of it every once in a while in your eyes."

"X-ray-vision time?" she joked, but her effort at levity sounded strained. "You don't want to take that Superman fantasy too far, you know. Your credibility might be questioned."

"Don't," he said, the edge in his voice sharp enough to cause puncture wounds. "I'm not asking you to tell me what happened. I just want you to know that I realize you've been to your own private hell and back."

Normally self-contained, Elizabeth didn't conceal

her feelings. She glared at him. He knew then that he'd hit a nerve. He felt a moment of satisfaction that Elizabeth the Calm was suddenly less calm. He no longer felt so out of control.

Michael saw hot sparks of pure fury light up her dark eyes. He sensed at that moment that she would be a volatile lover, and the thought of simply trying to hang on to her explosive passion made his pulse pick up speed and his groin swell. He silently cursed his body's poor timing and the public nature of their meeting place. He wanted to be alone with Elizabeth, as far from the prying eyes of the people strolling through the park and the nearby beach as possible. He wanted the freedom to hold her, to touch and explore her at his leisure whenever the spirit moved him.

"Is this where I'm supposed to make some kind of a confession?" she demanded in a tight little voice.

Michael didn't miss her fight for control. He grudgingly gave her high marks for her strength and poise. They were two of the qualities he enjoyed about her, but only up to a point. "Don't get all defensive on me. Confessions are between you and your priest, but it's been obvious since day one that you're learning how to trust yourself again." He saw the shock in her eyes.

She very carefully set aside her juice, then placed the bread on a napkin. "Why didn't you say any of this before tonight?"

He shrugged. Only Michael knew that the casual gesture was far less careless than it seemed. He realized what he was risking, but he felt the need to take the chance. He wanted more from her than she'd been willing to give so far. "You weren't ready to hear it."

"What makes you think I'm ready now?"

"You've said we're friends. And right now, *friend*, you need to trust someone."

He watched her struggle, watched her wrestle with the turmoil he'd sensed within her from the very beginning. He understood struggle, grasped the concept in ways she would never understand. Fingering the scar on his forehead, the result of an event that had nearly cost him his life, he suddenly felt a staggering array of emotions for Elizabeth Parker—emotions too far-reaching to describe, emotions that felt potentially threatening, emotions he'd never allowed himself to feel for another person in his entire adult life. His heart raced, as though to warn him that he couldn't control it much longer. Like his emotions, it was on the verge of breaking free.

"How did you know?"

The answer was tough to give, but he managed the job. By standing her ground with him, she'd given him the courage to share one of his secrets. "I've been there," he admitted, although the words hurt as he uttered them. "It takes time to heal. You can't afford to give up on yourself."

"I almost did."

He saw immediately how much the admission cost her. "Keep talking."

"The bad part was living with the fear that I'd been permanently robbed of my ability to feel. I was numb for a long time."

"Don't you realize that you're one of the most emotionally accessible people I've ever met? Hell! You're almost too accessible."

She smiled faintly. " 'Wearing your heart on your sleeve' is what my grandmother used to call it. I think it's a mixed blessing."

"There's nothing mixed about you, lady. Nothing at all. I meant it when I said not to change. You're a one-of-a-kind model."

"Thank you, I think," she said, her expression dubious.

"Don't thank me. It's my business to see the things that other people miss."

"I don't talk about the past," she cautioned, her chin lifting as her stubbornness resurfaced.

I don't either, he thought, *and look where it's gotten me.* He reminded her, "I haven't asked you to. Nor have I asked you what you did before you went back to school, although we both know your life didn't start two or three semesters ago. Maybe you're a widow. Maybe not. Maybe you're divorced and have ten kids. Maybe you had a business that went under, or maybe you just got out of prison. You might even be an ex–rocket scientist who was laid off and decided to make a career change. Somebody or something altered your life and destroyed your confidence. That much is clear. You'll tell me when you're ready."

"Maybe," she said very pointedly.

He didn't react to her deliberate use of his word.

Elizabeth reclaimed her juice. "I'm changing the subject now, so cooperate."

"Maybe," he answered just as pointedly, then took pleasure in the fact that she had to struggle to keep from smiling at him.

"If you couldn't direct documentaries, is there anything else you'd do?" She glanced at the platter of food on the bench between them, her bravado emerging in the form of another impudent question. "Have you considered a career in catering?"

He consciously sidestepped the urge to draw her into his arms and simply hold her. The restraint he employed almost killed him. Her strength was a given, but he knew she was bluffing just then. He ached for her, because it was obvious to him that she'd been betrayed by someone she'd trusted. Probably an ex-husband or a longtime lover. Eventually, he promised himself, he'd know the truth.

Glancing at the snack he'd assembled after placing an order with a local deli, Michael shrugged. "I'm just thorough."

"You're more than thorough, and we both know it. You're happiest when you're running things."

He didn't back away from her gently stated accusation. "Guilty."

"Still unrepentant, I see."

"Have I been a control freak with you?"

"Not until a few minutes ago. I have to admit that I've been surprised by your reserve."

He scowled at her, his expression emphasizing the hard angles of his face.

"I thought you'd push me much harder," she continued. "Even try to manipulate me, whether or not you really meant to. Some types of behavior are instinctive."

"Is that experience talking?"

She glanced away, and when she looked at him again her expression contained none of the alarm he'd first noticed. "My experience is based on surviving two older brothers who thought they could orchestrate my entire life for me. They could be very overpowering, but they taught me to hang on to my identity and my individuality with both hands."

Michael subjected her to a very thorough visual once-over before he spoke. Desire ran through him like a freight train at high speed. "I like your identity. I like it a whole lot," he muttered in a low voice.

"I like you too," Elizabeth said, that unexpected shyness and vulnerability emerging once again in her expressive features.

He searched her face, her eyes most of all. He saw all the way to her soul at times, and the view disconcerted him. She would expect more than physical intimacy from him. It was something he already knew about her, and he sensed that she would be disappointed by what she eventually found. A heart frozen in fear, a soul with a fist-size hole in it. A man willing to make love but not able to love. A man who viewed love as nothing more than an addiction, an addiction more powerful and far more destructive than those caused by designer drugs or alcohol.

"You're staring, Michael."

"Why aren't you married?" he asked, demand in his

tone. He wasn't sure why, but he suddenly needed an answer to that particular question.

She flinched, clearly startled. "I could ask the same question of you."

"I was engaged. A long time ago. It didn't work out. Now tell me about you," he commanded.

"I was engaged too."

"What happened?" Michael wondered about the fool who'd let her get away.

"Philosophical differences. They couldn't be bridged."

"That's wonderfully ambiguous," he scoffed.

"It's the truth. He didn't understand a decision I made. When I refused to reverse it, our relationship fell apart. I don't miss him. End of story." She fired each word at him with the steady precision of an expert shooter on a firing range.

He fired right back, unable, unwilling to give her any slack. "When?"

She paled. "Last year. Why is this so important to you?"

He ignored her question. "Are you really over him?" he asked, his tone intense.

"Of course I'm over him." Elizabeth stood suddenly. Facing him, she shoved her hands into her jacket pockets.

"Then why are you so upset right now?"

"I'm upset because you're behaving like a hammer. Verbally pounding on me stops now, Michael, or I'm out of here."

"You don't miss him? You don't want him back?"

"Absolutely not, to both questions. I don't mean to sound flip, but the relationship was destined to end. My family didn't understand a difficult choice I made last year, and neither did he."

Her silence prompted him to say, "Keep talking. You're not finished."

"Yes, I am finished, with him and with this conversation. This is none of your business."

He leaned forward and grabbed her arm as she paced in front of him.

She jerked free of him. "Don't."

"The marriage wouldn't have lasted," he said, his gaze narrowed as he watched her.

"No kidding." Elizabeth reclaimed her seat on the bench.

"You expect the traditions in a relationship, don't you?"

"Of course, as antiquated as that may sound to you or anyone else." After massaging her temples with her fingertips, she refocused on him. "Husband, kids, house, picket fence. I want the works. I think most people do, but there's a trick to doing it the right way."

Baffled by her last remark, he gestured impatiently. The director directing. "Explain."

"When you think you've fallen in love, you have to ask yourself one very simple question: Do you want to live your life without that person? The answer to the question is crucial. When I asked myself that question, the answer was an unqualified yes."

"He must have screwed up big-time."

"He did, but then, so did I. Now it's your turn," she

said, turning the tables on him with an adeptness he couldn't help admiring. "Why did your engagement end?"

Michael shrugged. "My work was more important to me than our relationship. When Cass recognized that reality, she declined to cope with it."

"She wanted the conventional?"

"She didn't want the totally unconventional. There's a difference."

Elizabeth nodded her understanding. "You didn't love her enough if you couldn't put her first at least part of the time."

"I cared, but I didn't love her." *I didn't want to love her*, he thought. *I don't want to love anyone.* "When she decided to move on, I encouraged her."

"Are you still friends?"

He nodded. "Good question. Stick with me, lady, and we'll turn you into a first-class interviewer."

"That's not an answer, Michael."

He touched one finger to his forehead in a mock salute. "I play racquetball with her husband when I have time, and I'm godfather to their twin sons."

She smiled. "That's wonderful."

He instantly warmed to the delight he saw in her eyes. "She's a good person. She didn't really deserve me."

"Her family gained a loyal and caring friend," she reminded him.

Elizabeth's vote of confidence caught him by surprise. He returned the favor by being more candid than usual. "You've been patient and supportive the past three weeks. That's meant a lot to me."

"You just needed a distraction."

"I needed to stop feeling sorry for myself," Michael admitted. "And you knew it. Thanks."

She smiled. "You're welcome, but I think we've helped each other. You were right a few minutes ago. I've needed a friend in recent months. When I reached out, you reached back. I'm glad," she finished quietly.

"Ditto." Michael leaned down and picked up the juice thermos. "Want a refill?"

She extended the empty cup. "Please."

He poured, his gaze on her heart-shaped face even after he set aside the thermos. He noticed the fatigue that shadowed her eyes. Once again he felt the urge to draw her into his arms and hold her. "Where are you?" he asked when she sighed.

She lifted her gaze from the contents of her cup. "Reflecting," she admitted.

"You can't change the past, so don't even try."

"Is that experience talking?" she asked.

Michael reluctantly nodded. The admission came with an astronomical price though. He remembered trying to change things as a boy. He'd failed. Now he knew to concentrate on only those things he could control. The rest he left alone. "You can't go back and change what's already happened, so don't try, Miss Lizzie. You'll only hurt yourself."

She managed a smile. "I don't any longer."

"Then quit torturing yourself." Even though he hadn't done the same, he realized.

She looked amused by his unceasing bossiness. Her amusement faded a moment later, though, and he saw the sadness that tinged her expression. "You really like your lone-wolf lifestyle, don't you?"

He considered telling her what most women wanted to hear, but honesty prevailed in the end. He owed her that much. "Yes, I do. And that's not going to change anytime soon."

She sighed, the sound weighted with emotions Michael didn't understand. "How's the editing coming along?"

He made himself move forward, made himself answer her. He refused to deal with the reason her missing smile bothered him so much. "Slow but steady. There's a lot of raw footage to deal with at this point in the process. The result happens when the material's been refined to the point that it possesses clarity and impact but lacks redundancy. It's easy to overmake your point, or to miss it entirely."

"Do you edit alone, or do you have a staff?"

"I do it alone, but only until I lose my perspective. Then I solicit input from people I've learned to trust over the years. I've never pretended to have all the creative answers, just the ones that relate to my vision of what the film should say."

"You have a lot of responsibility."

Michael chuckled. He wanted the responsibility, because dependence on others meant taking risks that went against the grain. He also couldn't help thinking about the outrageous amount of money he now earned.

If he lived to be a hundred, he'd never have time to spend it all. "I'm well compensated."

"That wasn't my point."

"No kidding."

She eyed him speculatively. "You don't trust people."

He grew very still for a moment. "Blunt, as always, I see."

"I'm not changing," she chirped right back at him with a neon-bright smile.

"You can count the people I really trust on the fingers of one hand."

"Who raised you?" she asked, a compassionate expression on her face.

"I pretty much raised myself."

"Where?" Her voice resonated with softness.

Looking grim, he shifted his gaze to the darkness that blanketed the coast. He hated remembering those years. "On the streets."

"Los Angeles?"

He nodded, his expression cast in stone to conceal the pain that still echoed within him.

"What about your parents?"

"Mismatched."

"It's difficult for a child when the parents don't get along."

"It's a common problem," he remarked dispassionately.

"You were a tough little guy, weren't you?"

He shrugged, the casual gesture a front. Michael remembered the constant fear that had driven him in those days. He remembered a mother in poor health, an actor father whose unrealized ambition had turned to resentment against a helpless wife and child, and the street thugs primed for violent retribution in a tough neighborhood if he made the mistake of stepping onto their turf. He remembered hunger as well when his father walked out and his mother's health failed and the welfare checks stopped coming. He remembered feeling helpless and powerless when he stood at her grave at the age of thirteen. And he remembered his vows never to need anyone and to succeed beyond anyone's wildest expectations, even his own. He remembered all of it. How could he forget?

"Michael . . . ?"

He lashed out. "Don't try to analyze me, Elizabeth."

"I'm not. I recognize the"—she paused—"the limitations of our friendship."

He understood her meaning, however delicate her phrasing. He understood it very well. "I'm the wrong man for your kind of woman."

She smiled sadly, but she said nothing more.

The gentleness shining from her eyes tore at him, made him feel as damaged on the inside as he knew he was. He told himself that he had every right to equate caring with loss. That had been his experience, and he'd learned from it. God, had he learned.

"What makes you laugh?" he asked, changing the subject because he was weary of being reminded of his past.

"That's easy. My older brothers when they think they're being subtle."

"What makes you cry?"

"Broken dreams."

"You're an idealist," he observed.

"Guilty, your honor."

"You have a tender heart."

She looked away then. "So I've been told."

"That wasn't an insult."

She glanced back at him, her dark eyes pools of emotional vulnerability. "I know."

"You love, don't you?" He watched the stillness that overtook her, then saw the start of a frown.

"Loving is like breathing, Michael. It's instinctive."

"Is it?" he asked, his heart suddenly feeling like a lump of cold lead in his chest. He knew about love, knew it trapped and destroyed. His parents had been living proof of that happy little ethic. *Change the subject*, he told himself. *This one is dangerous.*

"For me it is."

"Interesting perspective."

"Hardly, Michael," she said gently, her unwillingness to react to his cynicism obvious.

"Trust me, it is." Something—restraint, he guessed later when he thought about it—snapped inside him. He reacted defensively. He couldn't help himself. He felt crowded. "You're old enough to know that fairy tales are fiction."

She laughed, and it shocked him, shocked him enough to partially diffuse the unwieldy mixture of pain and anger inside him. He unclenched his fists, pressing his palms against the tops of his muscular thighs in an effort to completely calm himself.

She placed her fingers against her lips, trying not to let her laughter spill free. "I'm not laughing at you," she insisted when she could speak. "When you made that remark about fairy tales, I had a sudden mental image of Humpty Dumpty and no spare parts after his fall."

"I'll buy you a bucket of glue," he promised tersely.

Elizabeth looked at him then, really looked at him. He weathered her scrutiny, all the while wondering what was going through her mind. *Don't feel sorry for me*, he almost shouted when he saw what he thought might be pity in her eyes.

"But what shall we do about you? Glue won't work, will it, Michael?"

His jaw tightened, but he forced himself beyond her compassion. "Pretend I'm the Tin Man."

"But he had no heart!" she exclaimed.

"Right." The word slashed at the air between them like a sharp blade.

Michael saw the tears that welled in her eyes before she blinked them away. Dumbstruck, he stared at her. Tears? For him? He was a man who'd made women weep. He already knew that about himself. But he also knew that no one had wept for him since his thirteenth birthday.

He surged to his feet with the aid of his crutches, the need to distance himself from Elizabeth and his conflicted emotions acute. She stood, hastily setting aside her cup of juice.

"Michael . . ."

"Don't say anything," he ordered, furious with himself for losing control and with her for making him want things he knew were beyond his emotional reach. "You don't understand."

"Then help me to understand. Help me," she pleaded, moving toward him until the implacable expression on his face made her hesitate. "Michael, I want to understand."

He felt frozen, unable to move, unable to think clearly. She took a step in his direction, then another. He inhaled her fragrance even before she flowed against him, and, in the end, he couldn't resist what she offered. He felt like an addict, and she'd become his drug of choice.

Her arms slid around his waist and she molded herself to him. Michael shuddered, then embraced her. He immediately felt the love and comfort she offered, felt it right down to his shell of a soul. She was like a lifeline. He was the survivor who lacked the will to release her, even though he knew they'd both eventually drown. He loathed this weakness within himself that made him want her, but he stopped fighting it. He also stopped fighting her. He kenw then that his need for her would be his downfall. Hers as well.

FIVE

Carrying the supplies she'd assembled for a picnic supper with Michael, Elizabeth left her cottage just as dusk began to descend along the coastline. As she walked she noticed that more beachgoers than usual had lingered beyond the posted duty hours at the lifeguard towers. She assumed the hot August day had made people reluctant to depart the area, but she hoped that those who remained would exercise caution if they decided to indulge in night swimming.

Bypassing the entrance to Seagrove Park, Elizabeth cut across a well-lit public parking lot, her destination a sheltered strip of sand adjacent to the beach side of the park. She spread her blanket on the sand beside an empty firepit, unfolded a lawn chair for Michael, and then placed a square wicker basket in the center of the blanket. Kneeling beside it, she opened the top and quickly inventoried the contents to assure herself that she hadn't forgotten anything.

"I think it's my turn to be surprised."

Elizabeth glanced up to find Michael towering over her, his broad shoulders, flat belly, and muscular limbs displayed by the faded gym shorts and cropped T-shirt he wore.

"Join me," she invited breathlessly.

When he glanced questioningly at the lawn chair she'd placed at the edge of the blanket, she nodded, relieved that he hadn't seemed to notice her reaction to him. He carefully lowered himself into the chair, then propped his crutches against the cement rim of the firepit. His rugged features and broad smile enhanced Elizabeth's delight at his arrival.

"Very thoughtful," he remarked. "Thank you."

She heard an undercurrent of surprise in his voice, and she realized that this wasn't the first time she'd gotten the impression that Michael Cassidy found kindness from anyone unexpected. His reaction saddened her, but she kept her feelings to herself as she unpacked the contents of the wicker basket.

Since their emotional confrontation of a few nights before, she'd proceeded cautiously with Michael. Elizabeth knew in her heart that he needed her patience. Because she cared deeply about him, she refused to penalize him for his inability to express his emotions. She knew now that he kept his heart under lock and key because of something that had happened long ago. She wanted to believe that as trust flourished between them, he would feel able to open up to her. At least, she prayed he would. She felt his inner conflict as if it were her own, and she knew from experience the difficulty of talking about personal feelings.

"I thought a lawn chair made more sense than ordering a crane to haul you up from the blanket." She winked as she handed him a napkin and a bottle of imported beer. "There's a great local blues band playing tonight on the patio at Charlie's at the Beach, and this is the perfect spot for easy listening."

"Fine minds obviously think alike." Michael examined the label on the front of the beer she'd handed him. "Good choice. Your father and brothers trained you well, I see."

She scowled at his deliberate sexism. "I'll tell them you approve."

He removed the twist-off cap, raised the bottle to his lips, and took his first taste of the Danish beer. "I definitely approve," he said after he lowered the bottle, and his eyes skimmed over her shapely, tanned body, which was poorly concealed by her sunsuit.

Elizabeth felt confident about her appearance, so she thanked him with a smile as she reached for the remaining items stored in the bottom of the basket. Michael whistled appreciatively when she removed the lid of a large round plastic container and revealed the elaborate antipasto that she'd made.

"I've died and gone to heaven," he announced, his free hand placed with just the right amount of dramatic flare over his heart as he gazed at the results of her culinary efforts.

She smiled at his foolishness. "It's just a snack."

"The definition of a snack is three stale crackers, an

ounce and a half of old cheese, and a flat soda. This is a feast."

"I'm addicted to the deli at Daniel's Market," she confessed.

"Are we celebrating a meaningful event, or is this simply an example of your competence in the kitchen?"

Keep it simple, she told herself as she peered up at him. *Don't hand him your heart or your pride on a silver platter, and try not to admit to the man that every minute you spend with him feels like a gift that might be stolen away when you least expect it. You already know he wants you in his bed, because he hasn't made any secret of his desire. But that isn't love, and you'd hate settling for anything less than your dreams. Besides, if you tell him you're falling in love with him, or if you admit that you have this urge to spoil him with all the tenderness and thoughtfulness he's obviously missed in his life, he'll think you've lost your mind.*

Michael gave her a curious look. "Earth to Elizabeth. Come in, please."

Embarrassed by her lapse, she said, "We're celebrating life at the beach."

He lifted his beer, although his curious expression lingered. "To life at the beach, but only as long as it includes a friend."

She accepted his toast with a calm she didn't really feel, and sipped from the bottle of fruit juice she'd opened for herself. Although she felt the heat of Michael's gaze, Elizabeth concentrated on the task at hand. She spooned a generous portion of antipasto onto a plate, added a fork and a thick wedge of still-warm garlic bread, and then handed the masterpiece to

Michael. She assembled her own plate next, the portions more modest but just as inviting.

"As good as Gianotti's in West Hollywood," Michael declared, but only after sampling a slice of salami imported from Genoa, several plump black olives, and a chunk of fresh provolone cheese.

"I'll take that as a vote of approval." Grinning, she tasted a tart salad pepper and a paper-thin slice of Parma ham. "You're right. This is heaven."

"If you ever decide to go into the restaurant business, call me. I promise to be your first investor, provided I get all the free food I want."

"We have chocolate eclairs for dessert," she threw in just to tantalize his taste buds even more.

Michael groaned. "Be still, my heart."

She laughed out loud.

They talked as they ate their meal, their conversation filled with humor as they verbally wandered from the headlines in the morning paper to the judging criteria for documentary films at Cannes. Vowing that he had a hollow leg, Michael accepted second and third helpings of the antipasto.

Elizabeth ceased to be aware of anything or anyone but Michael, in spite of the people gathered around firepits, the blues tunes from Charlie's at the Beach carried on the faint breeze that had come up, and the others who periodically wandered past their tiny oasis. They completed their meal by sharing a calorie-rich eclair without a moment of remorse.

Seated beside Michael after she repacked the picnic basket, Elizabeth leaned against his uninjured leg and rested her head on his thigh as they chatted. His hand found its way to her shoulder, the rhythmic kneading of his strong fingers both soothing and seductive to her senses. She adored the feel of his hands on her body. Her skin tingled, and she felt more alive, more aware of everything around her. She also felt hungry for something more.

As she savored every stroke of his fingertips across her shoulder and up the side of her neck, she let her mind wander. She fantasized about his ability as a lover, his touch assuring her that he would be a skilled and generous partner. Worry nagged at her, because she wondered if he would ever be able to put his emotions on the line.

Somehow, she doubted it, and she promptly cautioned herself not to have unrealistic expectations of Michael. He'd already made it very clear that he had no room in his life for a woman who expected traditions like permanency or commitment.

"What was your childhood like?" he asked.

Although startled by his question, Elizabeth saw no point in pretending it hadn't been a happy time. "Secure. Hectic. Laughter-filled. Insane when my brothers were adolescents. Pretty normal, I suspect." *Things are different now*, she reflected, *so it's best to remember the good times*.

Gazing up at the star-bright night sky, she continued. "My parents still live in the house where I grew up. They bought it when they first moved to San Diego. It was a shoebox in those days, but it was a Craftsman shoebox, so the quality of the dwelling was a given. They've expanded several times over the years, adding a second story that has three extra bedrooms, putting in a great room, expanding the kitchen, that sort of thing, but without destroying the integrity of the design. My father was trained as a carpenter before he went into law enforcement, so he's done most of the work himself."

"He sounds"—Michael paused, clearly searching for the right description—"solid and reliable."

What a telling choice of words, Elizabeth thought as she nodded. "He is, but in a very low-key sort of way. He leads by example, and he tends to be very modest. In fact, he rarely calls attention to himself. I personally think he's shy. Mother has always been the gregarious one. She taught school for almost thirty years. We have barbecues almost every other weekend when they aren't off RVing. You'll have to join us when the whole gang gets together. There's lots of laughter, mountains of food, and we play touch football in the backyard."

Turning, she peered at Michael. Despite the limited illumination from a nearby streetlight, she didn't have to wonder how he felt. His bleak expression spoke volumes.

He returned her gaze, studying her upturned face for several moments before admitting, "I can't relate on a personal level to what you're talking about, although I've seen that kind of parenting with friends and their children, so I know some people are actually capable of it."

His honesty humbled her. It also made her want to weep for him. "It's a matter of taking time for your children and being consistent with them. It's also a matter of loving, listening, establishing boundaries, and offering guidance to them. Children deserve to know that they can always depend on the adults who are raising them. That, in my humble opinion, is good parenting."

Michael looked away. Elizabeth followed his gaze to the pinpoint-size string of lights shining on the distant horizon. She knew from countless months of sleepless nights the previous year that the lights marked a vessel that was either an oil tanker or a transport ship. Glancing back at him, she watched him finger the scar above his left eyebrow. Shaped like an inverted boomerang, it was narrow and pale. She suspected that it was a symbol of an event replete with emotional pain. She sensed, as well, that Michael touched it as a response to some kind of need to remind himself not to place his emotions in jeopardy, not to risk his heart. It occurred to her then that they both were dealing with emotional risk, although for very different reasons.

"You always do that when you're in a reflective mood."

His fingers stilled. "Do what?"

"You touch the scar on your forehead. How did it happen?"

Lowering his hand, he flattened it palm down against his thigh. "An accident when I was a kid."

"Tell me about it," she encouraged.

"It's not something I usually talk about."

"I know," she said quietly. "But would you make an exception for me?"

Michael exhaled as he settled back in his chair. "I took a fall down a flight of stairs when I was eleven. This was the result."

"Were you hospitalized?"

He nodded. "For several weeks."

"Your injuries must have been very serious."

He shifted restlessly. "I didn't regain consciousness for a while."

"Your mother must have been terribly worried."

"She was bedridden by then."

"And your father?"

"He'd already left."

His emotionless presentation of the facts of a life-changing childhood event tugged at her heart and validated what she already realized. Michael concealed his feelings better than anyone she'd ever known. "So you were on your own even then?" she confirmed as she struggled to keep her expression neutral.

He shrugged. "Pretty much on my own. A neighbor helped out. It really doesn't matter. This is all ancient history, and I don't need a shrink."

She noted the sharp edge in his voice. "I'm not trying to play shrink, Michael. I wouldn't do that to you."

"Then why all the questions?"

"I'm guilty of curiosity, but it isn't idle." When he didn't say anything, she reminded him, "I've answered all the questions you've asked me."

"Not all of them."

She looked away, aware that he was right. She felt like a fake at moments like these. What would he think of her once he discovered that her self-confidence was a façade?

"You don't want to know everything there is to know about me, Elizabeth."

"Sharing is important."

"So is privacy," he countered, his voice tight with tension, his fists clenched atop his muscular thighs. "There are some things in a person's life that are no one's business."

She suddenly needed to touch him. Taking one of his hands, she peeled back his fingers and placed her smaller one over his so that their palms met. "Forgive me for prying?" she asked.

He pulled her up to her knees without warning. As she knelt between his thighs and peered up at him, he cupped her heart-shaped face. She felt her pulse speed up, but she didn't pull away, not even when he drove his fingers into the thick mane that crowned her head. Her eyes fell closed, her lips parting as she sucked air into her lungs. She absorbed the tempered strength in the flexing of his fingers and in the musculature of his thighs as they pressed against her ribs. She opened her eyes, her gaze sweeping over his face. He had the most sensual mouth. A mouth she longed to taste.

"I've never met anyone like you."

Trembling with desire, she jerked herself free of the fantasy that had momentarily held her in thrall. She smiled, unaware of the fragility of her expression. "Then we're even." Could anyone heal his damaged heart? she wondered. Could *she*, when her own heart was in such turmoil? Turning her head, she pressed a kiss into his palm, the gesture more spontaneous than planned. Elizabeth saw his shock.

"Why?" he asked, his voice ragged.

"Why not?" she answered, acutely aware of the need within to express her emotions. "You aren't blind or deaf, Michael. You know I care about you."

"There's no future in it," he said sharply.

"You're wrong," she insisted just as sharply. "There will always be a future for two people when they are friends. And it's all right if we never become anything more."

"All right?" he demanded, a flash of hurt in his hazel eyes before he blinked it away.

Hope sparked in her heart, but she didn't let herself dwell on this unexpected chink in Michael's armor. "Wrong choice of words. I can adjust if we never become anything more than friends, but only because that's what you need from me. I care enough about you not to manipulate or trap you, but I also care enough about myself not to volunteer for heartache."

His fingers, still buried in her thick hair, spasmed, then grew gentle again. Elizabeth arched under his touch, savoring the feel of his fingers as he slid them over her scalp and massaged away the tension of the day. But he aroused other tensions. Inner tensions that made her aware of her body's hunger for him. She closed her eyes and let herself float, hands gripping his powerful thighs, fingertips kneading the muscles there with a decidedly feline rhythm.

"Why do you trust me?" he demanded several minutes later.

She sighed, although she didn't open her eyes. "Is there some reason I shouldn't?"

"Give me an answer," he insisted.

"All right." She blinked, refocusing on Michael's night-shadowed features. "I trust you because you have integrity."

He swore, the word an anger-filled exhalation of air as it passed his lips. "What are you trying to do to me? Endow me with the character traits of some damn saint?"

Was that Michael speaking? Was the man with the splintered-sounding voice really him? She started to ease backward, but he thwarted her effort to free herself by clamping down on her shoulders with both hands. He didn't hurt her, though, and she knew he never would.

"Talk to me, Elizabeth."

"I'm not *trying* to do anything. I'm just feeling my way along, attempting to be a good friend. That's all."

"I don't talk about the past because there's nothing back there that I want to remember. It's that simple."

Or that complicated, she thought to herself.

He began to massage her shoulders again, his touch gentle.

"When do your classes begin?" he asked several moments later.

My classes? What a question! she thought as she grappled with the upended feeling he'd caused. "In about four weeks."

"Nervous?"

She shook her head, trying to clear away the dense

haze of desire consuming her senses. "Not really. I've gotten a head start on my thesis research, and I've done most of the reading for my classes. I thought I'd better get ahead since I'll be teaching some of the lower division classes, and I won't have as much study time as I've had in the past."

He cupped her chin with one hand. "You're starting to look more rested. The shadows under your eyes have faded."

Disconcerted by his thoroughness, she ducked free. "I've been very lazy the last few days."

"You've earned the time off."

Glancing at him, she smiled. "The worst is over."

"But only temporarily."

She nodded. Denying the truth would have been stupid. Her goal hadn't changed, and it wouldn't. She intended to complete her advanced degree in under the allotted time. She had the blessings of the department chairman, but she knew she still faced an uphill battle. It was a battle she intended to win though. "I plan to enjoy every single minute of the rest of the summer break."

"Does that mean we'll see each other during the daylight hours?"

She laughed. "If only to prove to ourselves that we're not Dracula's minions. You have to admit that three and a half weeks of nightly encounters on a park bench is a bit odd."

"I dream about you at night."

Startled, she stared at him. The desire she glimpsed in his eyes unnerved her. "More nightmares, huh?" she teased as she tried to bank the desire pooling deep inside of her body.

"You don't give me nightmares, Elizabeth. You never have."

"I'll trust you on that."

"You don't want to know about my dreams?"

She nibbled on her lower lip for a moment while she considered how to answer his question. In the end she didn't bother with the flippant comments that came to mind. "I'm a little curious."

He leaned forward. She held very still.

"I think about what it would be like to make love to you," he said very softly.

She felt her heart stutter to a stop in her chest. "Michael . . ."

"Don't pretend to be surprised."

"I'm not . . . I mean, I won't. The truth is, I've thought about what it would be like between us too."

"And?"

"Utterly memorable," she whispered. The hunger she felt for him was reflected in the accelerated pace of her heart and the heat steaming through her veins.

"Now what do we do?" he asked. "Pretend we're both not wondering what it would be like to be lovers?"

"I don't know how to answer you."

She eased free of him. His hands fell away from her shoulders. Reaching up, she stroked the side of his face with her fingertips. She trembled when he captured her hand, turned his head, and pressed a kiss into the center of his palm. "Wanting you isn't enough for me, Michael. I've never made a secret of my expectations in a relationship. I couldn't be casual with you. I care about you."

He swore, but this time the word wasn't an angry hiss. It was, instead, a sound that resonated with regret and loss. "I like your honesty, but it's a double-edged sword some of the time."

Flustered, she said, "You've got to be the only man I've ever known who thinks my bluntness is a character asset."

"It's part of who you are. I happen to approve of the entire package." His gaze dipped to the V of her sun-suit, and a tuneless little whistle escaped him as he viewed the cleavage revealed there.

"The package thanks you," she quipped, the heat of her desire for him and her instinctive humor sparkling in her eyes. "I guess I've never known anyone who didn't feel threatened by the fact that I have a mind and like to use it."

"Secure men don't play those games."

"Can I quote you? My brothers definitely need a new role model. So do a few other people I can think of right off the top of my head."

"You're talking about your ex-fiancé, aren't you?"

"Unfortunately. Like a lot of people, he tried to control things. It wore on my nerves after a while."

"Foolish man."

"In the end, I thought so too," she said.

"When you think about making love, do you like the thoughts you have about us?"

Because his question was direct, Elizabeth saw no

point in playing games. "Yes, but I still won't have a casual affair with you, Michael."

"You expect more than any man can reasonably promise."

She smiled, and she sounded far calmer than she actually felt as she spoke. "That's a matter of opinion, and you have a right to yours."

He exhaled, the sound suspiciously melodramatic. "You're not going to debate this with me, are you?"

"Nope, but I'd say yes to a hug."

He smiled. "They broke the mold with you, Miss Lizzie." He opened his arms to her. "Come here, then."

Elizabeth accepted his invitation. As he held her, she savored Michael's strength and the honor he didn't seem to know he possessed. She also mourned his unwillingness to love as her desire for him scorched her heart and seared her soul.

SIX

The state of California had arranged that John Mason be buried in the equivalent of a pauper's grave. A headstone gave his name and the year in which his life had ended. Nothing more.

Elizabeth knew the facts though. A man had died. The bullet had come from her gun, but the choice had been his. He'd chosen to rob a bank. He'd chosen to try to end her life by firing his weapon at her. He'd also chosen to cripple her partner.

As she stood there, she reflected on the incident that would forever link her to John Mason. She'd come to the cemetery with the hope of achieving some sense of closure, not to punish herself. Although forever changed by the reality that she'd been forced to shoot him in the line of duty, she knew now that John Mason had been the architect of his own demise. She'd simply been the unwitting accomplice.

In truth, she'd mourned his loss for reasons that had

little to do with his actual death. Although emotionally shaken because it was her first—and would be her only —visit to his grave, Elizabeth found a measure of comfort in the knowledge that she'd done her best in an impossible situation. She didn't feel guilt. What she felt had more to do with relief that she'd survived an event that had altered her perceptions of herself, ended her career, and damaged her family relationships.

She walked away from the unadorned gravesite a few minutes later, a silent prayer whispering through her mind for inner peace. She'd worked hard to survive the emotional trauma of the shooting, but she knew in her heart that she still had more work to do. She rededicated herself to the task as she made her way to the parking lot at the edge of the cemetery. She realized, as well, that it was time to tell Michael what had happened. Although she hadn't figured out exactly how to broach the subject with him, she refused to avoid the inevitable any longer. She told herself that she was ready for his reaction to the truth, whatever it might be. She hoped she wasn't lying to herself.

Her steps faltered when she heard the distinctive sound of motorcycle engines. Glancing toward the entrance to the parking lot, she spotted two men she instantly recognized, although both wore helmets that concealed their faces. Elizabeth exhaled, the sound a heavy gust of resignation as it left her body. She resolutely made her way to her car, aware that both men were there to see her.

"Why do this to yourself, baby sister?" Tom Parker demanded as he parked his motorcycle and jerked off his helmet. The more assertive of her two brothers, he normally controlled his short temper, but not today.

"Why do what, Tommy?" she asked, pride giving her voice strength.

"Beth . . ." Mark began.

She flashed a look at her other brother, who immediately fell silent. Mark was the more conciliatory of the two, although Elizabeth noticed that his expression was filled with similar disapproval. "Don't interfere, Mark."

"Answer me, baby sister. What the hell are you doing here?"

"I don't owe you an explanation."

Tom swore.

Elizabeth ignored his anger.

Mark left his helmet on the seat of his motorcycle and approached her. "Need a hug?"

She almost smiled. "Only if you keep your opinions to yourself when you're giving it to me."

"Deal, kiddo. You already know how I feel, and I don't see the point in repeating myself."

She welcomed his powerful bear hug, and discovered that it did a lot to ease the residual sadness that had settled over her since her arrival at the cemetery.

Tom approached his brother, younger by four years, and his sister, younger still by eight. "You were a fool to let some dead guy drive you off the force. You can still go back, so why the hell don't you?"

"He didn't drive me off the force. I made a decision. Unfortunately, none of you respects it."

"This isn't about respect," Mark insisted, his arm still looped around her shoulders.

Elizabeth eased free of him, digging into the pocket of her slacks as she walked away from her two brothers. They followed her, their booted feet making a distinctive sound on the pavement. She knew they felt protective of her, but she also knew that all the explanations in the world wouldn't change their conviction that she'd behaved like a coward when she'd resigned from the department.

"Don't be stubborn, Beth," counseled Mark. "Talk to us."

Her own temper surfaced. She turned to face them after unlocking and opening her car door. "I've talked to all of you until I'm blue in the face. I'm not willing to argue the point any further. If I go back to the department, it'll be on my terms, but never as a uniformed officer. That's the way it is. Adjust. I have."

"You're scared," Tom accused her.

"You're right, I am. I'm afraid I'll hesitate at the wrong moment, and someone else might die."

"It won't happen. You've got more grit than that."

Tears suddenly filled her eyes. "I've got enough grit not to jeopardize other people. Has that ever occurred to either one of you, or to Dad? Why can't any of you understand the strength it took to see the potential for disaster and then admit it to myself? Why, dammit! Why?"

Mark moved in her direction. "Beth, don't leave."

She shook her head. "I have to. Sorry. Take care, both of you."

"Elizabeth!"

She smiled sadly, her vision blurred by emotion as

she tossed her purse into her car. "You sound just like Daddy, Tom."

Because she knew they didn't intend to answer the questions she'd asked, she got into the vehicle, shoved the key into the ignition, and backed out of her space. She glanced in the rearview mirror once she blinked back her tears. She saw the two brothers she adored, the two brothers who'd managed to upset her far more than her decision to visit the grave of John Mason, attempted murderer and bank robber.

Michael seriously doubted that anyone who knew him would ever make the mistake of referring to him as a patient man. Intolerant. Temperamental. Exacting. Bullheaded. Now, those were the words he recalled hearing most frequently. He paid little attention to the opinions of others, though, and he made it a rule never to apologize to anyone for his character or his personal style. Ego aside, he simply had better things to do with his time.

In recent weeks, however, he'd discovered within himself the capacity for a slightly more mellow attitude. He gave Elizabeth credit for the change. Unfortunately, what little tolerance he'd managed to acquire was rapidly evaporating as he watched her stare off into space. This was not the scenario he'd envisioned when he'd asked her to spend the afternoon with him.

He felt stirrings of genuine concern, and of his infamous temper, as he watched her now. Elizabeth's demeanor hadn't changed for the better part of an hour.

Michael wanted to understand the cause of her monosyllabic replies and uncharacteristic self-absorption, even though he sensed that persuading her to talk would be a major undertaking. He decided to try anyway.

"Care to tell me what's wrong with you today?" he asked.

She flinched, glancing briefly at him before her gaze shifted back to the colorful windsock suspended from the upper balcony of the sprawling beachfront house. The six-foot-long expanse of multicolored silk bounced and bobbed on currents of sea air.

He frowned. "Elizabeth?"

"Nothing's wrong."

Seated at an umbrella-shaded table on the rear patio of the Buckmans' retreat, Michael leaned back in his chair. He appeared to be far calmer than he actually felt. The tinted lenses of the aviator-style sunglasses he wore shielded his eyes from the sun and concealed his concern. "You're a lousy liar."

Elizabeth reached for her purse, which she'd placed on the redwood deck beside her chair. "I've got errands to run. Why don't I stop by later, and we . . ."

He caught her by the wrist, effectively halting her rise from the chair. What little patience he possessed disappeared altogether. "Sit down and tell me what the hell's wrong with you. You haven't said ten civil words in the last hour."

Jerking her arm free, she glared at him as she sank back down into her chair. "Do not play director with me. I don't appreciate being ordered around."

He refused to rise to the bait of her flaring temper. "For the record, I'm not *playing* at anything. You're upset, and we both know it. Tell me why."

"I don't want to talk about it right now."

"Who died?" he asked. Because Michael knew her humor had an exceedingly irreverent side to it, his tone and his words were deliberately flippant. He intended to jump-start her into a good mood, but the reaction he got wasn't at all what he anticipated.

Elizabeth grew so pale, she looked on the verge of fainting. When she raised a shaking hand to her temple and pressed her fingertips to the pulse there, Michael felt like a thug who went around kicking puppies. He knew something was terribly wrong. He spoke again, but with far greater care this time. "Has something happened to your parents?"

Obviously startled by his question, she lowered her hand to her lap. "Of course not. They're still vacationing in Alaska."

He thought then about the brothers she adored, the brothers who teased her unmercifully, the brothers who'd helped her, along with her father, to restore the once-run-down beach cottage she now called home, the same brothers who faced mean city streets every time they donned their uniforms and went out to preserve and protect. Surely she would have told him if something had happened to one of them.

"Are your brothers all right, Elizabeth?"

"They're fine. I saw them both this . . . morning."

Noting her hesitation, not just the discordant note

in her voice, he pursued the lead she'd provided. "Where were they when you saw them?"

She shook her head, her expression shuttering closed. "It doesn't matter."

"I think it does." He extended his hand, a simple gesture that expressed his hope that she would meet him halfway. "I think it matters a whole lot, Miss Lizzie."

She frowned at him, and he didn't pretend not to understand why. No matter how much it annoyed her, she let him get away with the nickname he'd given her during their first days together. He noticed that his use of it now seemed to cause a small crack in the otherwise seamless wall she'd constructed around her emotions. Michael saw, as well, her struggle for control. His gaze narrowed. She looked worried and afraid.

Afraid of what? he wondered. *What had Elizabeth so worried?* She seemed almost fearless at times, and she rarely shut him out. Her reluctance to trust him now wounded his pride and set every instinct for jeopardy that he possessed on full alert, while her emotional distance, so out of character for the woman he'd come to know, sent a chill across his soul.

He watched her stare at his hand. He kept it extended in her direction, refusing to give up on her. "Reach back," he urged, his voice low, steady, and very determined as he used the same words she'd once employed to describe the start of their friendship.

She glanced at him, her uncertainty apparent. Michael didn't move a muscle. Regaining her trust became his focus, and he didn't intend to give up without a fight.

Elizabeth responded without warning. *Finally*, he thought. The instant their fingertips touched, tears flooded her eyes.

"Talk to me," he urged, his grip on her both possessive and protective as he reacted to her obvious distress. "Tell me what's happened."

She inhaled, pulling enough air into her body to steady herself, but not pulling away from him. "I can't. Not yet anyway."

"Why?"

Lifting her chin, she managed a watery smile. "I don't want to fall apart all over you."

Michael understood the extent of her pride. It was a character trait they shared, but he wanted her to trust him enough to lean on him.

"For God's sake, Elizabeth, talk to me. I don't care if you fall apart," he assured her. Impatiently removing his sunglasses with his free hand, he tossed them onto the table. "Just this once, of course."

Elizabeth looked directly at him. Her chin trembled. "I mind, dammit. I mind a whole lot."

He eased his fingers through hers in a loose weave. "I'm not letting go of you until you talk to me."

She exhaled, the sound ragged enough to tear at his insides. He watched her pick at the frayed bottom of the T-shirt she wore over her bathing suit. Her hair, swept away from her face by a terry headband, resembled a dark halo and emphasized how pale she'd become.

He summoned all the patience he possessed, patience he hadn't been aware of until his relationship with Elizabeth began. It occurred to him then that she'd fostered numerous new emotions and responses within him in their short time together. "Your secrets are safe with me."

She nodded. "I know. You're—" She paused abruptly, her struggle to control her emotions evident.

"I'm what?" he encouraged.

"You're the only person I've been able to relax with in a long time."

Michael knew she was close to her family, knew how tight knit a group they were. *What kind of crisis had kept her from turning to them?* he wondered. "What about your family?" he asked, wanting to understand the cause of the rift.

"I can't."

"That's your pride talking. You've given me the impression that they rally around their own in time of crisis."

She nodded. "They normally do, but not this time."

He tried another approach when he saw her eyes fill again. "Has something happened to one of your friends?"

"Something happened to a friend, but it was about a year ago."

"That's a long time," he remarked.

She shook her head, unexpected vehemence in the gesture. "No," she insisted. "It's not long at all. Sometimes it feels like yesterday."

"Why, Elizabeth?"

"It was the night I shot a man."

He stared at her, shock reverberating inside him. "Say that again. I don't think I heard you correctly."

With an eerie calm she did as he asked. "I shot a man, Michael."

"Why?"

"To keep him from killing my partner." Almost as an afterthought, she added, "And me."

Partner? "Where were you?"

"At a bank."

Michael watched her lift her hand and press her fingertips to her forehead again. As much as he wanted her to continue with her explanation, he could almost feel the pain reflected in her eyes. "Do you want something for that headache?"

Sagging back in her chair, she nodded. "Please."

He reached for his crutches, which he'd left propped against the patio table. Getting up from his chair, he made short work of retrieving a bottle of aspirin from a cupboard in the kitchen. He paused beside Elizabeth when he returned to the patio.

"One or two?" he asked.

"Two, please."

Seated in his chair a few minutes later, he reached out to her at the same moment that she extended her hand to him.

"I'm sorry."

"What the hell for?" he asked, his frustration surfacing.

"For being such a baby." She gave him a weary

look. "I'm a fake, Michael. I'm not the person you think I am."

"You aren't making any sense."

"I'm making perfect sense!" she exclaimed. "You don't know the real me. My family thinks I'm a coward. Maybe I am."

"Tell me exactly what happened. And start at the beginning, Miss Lizzie, because this isn't going to make any sense to me if you don't."

She nodded. "I was a police officer for eleven years."

Shocked a second time, Michael stared at her.

She smiled wanly. "I'd never used my gun until that night. Not once. Despite what people think about cops, we don't go around playing shoot-'em-up."

"You told me your family thought a career in law enforcement was a lousy idea for you," he reminded her, still reeling from her revelation.

"They did. The consensus was that I had the smarts and the discipline, but that it would be impossible for me to survive the emotional stresses of the career. They all disapproved of my decision when I joined the police department." Her voice shook as she spoke. "They all think of me as some kind of emotional marshmallow."

"You're the baby," he said, speculating aloud because she'd shared so much information about her family that he felt as though he knew them all. "They feel protective where you're concerned."

Sparks of fury flashed in her eyes. "I'm an adult, Michael. A thirty-four-year-old adult."

"You don't have to convince me," he assured her,

relieved to see some evidence of her feisty nature again. "I was just thinking out loud, trying to see you from their perspective. Is it fair to assume that the shooting validated their feelings?"

She nodded. "I suspect so, but that's not a subject I'll discuss with any of them."

"Things aren't right with them?" he clarified.

"Things are a mess."

"Why?"

"I've always tried to respect their opinions, but that didn't stop me from making the career choice that worked for me. I was good at my job, Michael. Very good. I was a member of a special police task force assigned to predominantly low-income neighborhoods. I developed skills as a mediator in domestic disputes, and I also worked with young people who were vulnerable to a lot of performance pressure by the gangs. My brothers and my father were surprised by how well I did, and they finally came around." She met his gaze, her expressive eyes filled with emotion and pride. "No one ever filed a complaint against me, not once in eleven years. My personnel file is filled with commendations attesting to the high standards I demanded of myself. Now my family's ashamed of me. They act as though I betrayed them when I left the department."

He hated the fact that her confidence had been so badly shaken that she felt compelled to defend herself even now, but he still didn't understand the specifics of the situation she'd faced the previous year. "You said you shot someone. What exactly happened?"

She exhaled, the sound ragged enough to make Michael's heart ache. He wanted to draw her into his arms. He restrained himself though, because he sensed that sympathy was the last thing Elizabeth wanted or needed at the moment.

"A silent alarm went off at the main branch of a local bank. My partner and I were off duty, but he had a radio in his car. We responded to a robbery-in-progress call. We were only a block away. It was late, after midnight on a Friday. You're familiar with the inner city streets, so you know personnel can get stretched pretty thinly across a metropolitan area on a weekend night."

Michael nodded. He did understand, having spent countless hours with film crews and undercover officers in various cities across the country over the years.

"Rod and I were the first ones to arrive at the bank. The robbery was still going down. We found a rent-a-cop in the parking lot behind the building. He'd taken a bullet in the chest, and was unconscious. After requesting backup and an ambulance, both code two so that we wouldn't alert anyone to our presence, we decided to investigate before the other units arrived. The building was huge, so we split up once we got inside."

She paused, reaching again for her water glass. Michael saw the tremors that went through her hand, then the white-knuckled grip that followed as she took a drink.

Michael already grasped the extent of the strength and courage required of anyone in law enforcement, whether male or female. In simple terms, it was a grueling job that took a heavy toll. Elizabeth lacked the jaded cynicism of the experienced cops he'd encountered, and he found it hard to believe she'd endured the pressure-cooker lifestyle for eleven years. Although he kept his opinion to himself, he agreed with her family. He considered her too tenderhearted to survive over the long term the pressures inherent in the work, and he felt genuine relief that she'd left the profession, regardless of the motivation that had led her to the decision.

"You okay?" he asked.

She nodded. "I'm better. Thanks for listening. I've never discussed this with anyone outside the department."

"You're not finished," he said, his voice quiet but firm.

She looked away, her gaze straying to their joined hands. He squeezed her fingers, reassurance in the simple gesture. She smiled so tremulously, Michael felt even more protective of her. No one had ever inspired these feelings in him, and he felt a moment of unease.

"The situation started to fall apart after we located the guy who'd blown the safe door," Elizabeth went on. "Unarmed, he was mumbling to himself and frantically stuffing money into a duffel bag. He acted like he was high on something. Rod and I had communicated by radio as we'd searched the building, and neither one of us had seen evidence of an accomplice. When we saw this clown standing in the vault, we thought . . . well, you can imagine what we thought. We believed that we'd lucked out and nailed the sole perp in a bank robbery. We were totally unprepared when some guy wearing a ski mask charged us from behind. He suddenly started shooting. Rod dropped like a rock. At the time, I thought he was dead." She paled, but she kept talking, although her husky voice was even more emotionally revealing than usual. "I immediately dove for cover behind a file cabinet. The guy in the walk-in safe went berserk, throwing clumps of money at the shooter and screaming that no one was supposed to get hurt. Meantime, his partner pointed his gun at me, because I was still partially exposed. He fired once. I fired back. My round took him down. Even though he was wounded, he pointed his weapon at me once again." She shuddered, but made herself continue. "I fired a second time. I learned later that his gun had jammed."

"What you're telling me is that in the line of duty you shot a man in self-defense, Elizabeth."

She met his gaze and nodded. "That's precisely what I'm telling you."

"It's unfortunate, but you obviously had no other option."

She nodded. "I know that, Michael. I've always known that. It's just that the man died . . . four weeks later. And today was the first anniversary of his death."

He felt nothing but contempt for the unknown criminal who'd tried to kill her, so he reacted with his usual bluntness. "I'm just glad it wasn't you."

"So am I," she said, as honest and direct as always.

Michael felt relieved. He'd feared that she'd been experiencing some misguided sense of guilt, not just understandable regret over the tragedy that had taken place. "What about your partner?"

Closing her eyes, she rubbed her forehead. "Rod

will be in a wheelchair for the rest of his life. He's paralyzed from the waist down."

"Rotten luck, but hardly your fault," he reminded her.

"I know that too. I went into counseling in order to work through all the emotions that follow a fatal shooting incident, and I've come to terms with most of it, I think."

His gaze narrowed suddenly. "You said the guy shot at you."

Her expression became guarded. "Yes."

"He didn't miss, did he?"

"No, he didn't miss, but it wasn't a serious wound."

"You were shot, and you don't consider the event serious? Dammit, Elizabeth!"

She winced. "Don't, please. You sound like my father and brothers when you react that way. It was minor, a flesh wound. Although it bled a lot, no real damage was done."

The real damage, Michael decided, was less visible. Her confidence had obviously been battered. He hadn't known just how right he'd been when he'd told her that she was learning to trust herself again. He did comprehend, however, how damaging self-doubt could be. He'd mistakenly believed that her moments of emotional vulnerability were based on a failed love affair. He knew now that he couldn't have been more wrong.

"Where were you hit?" he asked.

"My rib cage." She touched a spot about four inches beneath her right armpit. "I have a small scar."

"Now for the hard question. Did you resign, or were you dismissed from the department?"

Her chin came up a fraction of an inch. "I resigned of my own accord, and only after Internal Affairs conducted a thorough investigation. The shooting was ruled justified," she said. "I waited to resign until the investigation was over, as much for my sake as for my grandfather, my father, and my two brothers. I also made very sure the media and my fellow officers knew the outcome of the investigation, because I didn't want any family reputations tainted by the decisions I made."

He whistled in surprise. "You're third generation?"

"I was," she said with quiet dignity. "My brothers have that distinction now."

"You intend to go back, don't you?"

She shook her head. "I'll never go back into uniform. I wouldn't jeopardize another officer that way."

He frowned, then realized a few moments later exactly what she meant. "You aren't sure you could use your weapon a second time."

"Exactly, so I won't take the risk, Michael. Hesitation is potentially deadly if it happens at the wrong time."

"I understand," he said.

"Then you're the only person who does."

"What do you mean?"

Elizabeth sighed. "My family and my fiancé kept telling me to get back on the horse that had thrown me. They didn't understand—they still don't understand—that the risk is too great. I honestly doubt my ability to use my weapon again. Besides, we're not talking about horses; we're talking about people's lives. If I hesitate, even for a split second, then someone might die. I cannot take that risk. I *won't* take it. Not ever."

He exhaled, torn between hating that she'd been deprived of her dream and relief that she wouldn't ever face the uncertainty and danger of the city streets again. "When I asked if you planned to go back, I was thinking more along the lines of your working as a department psychologist. Having a former cop in that job benefits everyone concerned. You'd be a natural."

She nodded, her expression still somewhat wary. "That's my plan. And, perhaps, crisis intervention when I'm ready for it."

Michael's gaze narrowed. "Talk to me, Miss Lizzie. Don't make me play can opener again. There's something you've left out. I can feel it."

"Your directorial instincts are showing," Elizabeth chided.

He felt encouraged by her faint smile. "Really? So give. What's the missing piece of this puzzle?"

She sighed. "The part that takes the longest to heal. The fact that someone died. Although I know I did exactly what I was supposed to do in the situation at the bank, it still hurts that a life was lost."

Michael understood the dilemma she faced. "You value human life, so it damn well should have hurt. There'd be something wrong with you if you didn't hurt. Unfortunately, you were forced to make a split-second decision based on your training and experience. I think you made the only reasonable choice under the circumstances, and I'm glad you're still alive, so please don't let it haunt you."

"I agree with you." After a moment's hesitation, she confessed, "I was so furious with that man after he died. At first I thought I'd lost my mind to be angry at a dead man, but he robbed me of my options. He didn't care that I went into law enforcement to save lives, and he didn't care that he crippled my partner."

Michael swore, the word as rancorous as the rage he felt that someone had upended her world and filled her with self-doubt. He knew from personal experience just how damaging that emotion could be. He also understood the struggle to move beyond that kind of a personal crisis. Not everyone succeeded. He knew he hadn't, at least not completely.

"Where'd you go this morning?" Michael asked, still curious about how her brothers figured into the equation.

"The cemetery."

"Why?" he demanded.

"You're overreacting," she said. "I went there to put this episode to rest once and for all. I didn't go to the cemetery for any other reason, because I know in my heart that I didn't do anything legally or morally wrong."

"Were your brothers with you?"

She nodded. "They arrived just as I was leaving."

"What happened?"

"They refuse to understand why I resigned. They can't get it into their heads that it was harder to walk away than to stay with the department. When Tom and

Mark tried to talk me into going back into uniform, I lost my temper and left."

"How'd they know you were there?"

She sighed softly. "They know me too well."

"Sounds like it." He fell silent for a moment. "I don't get it. They should understand the situation and your decision better than most people."

"They should, but they don't, and they can't be objective where I'm concerned. Neither can my father."

"They care about you, or they wouldn't have shown up at the cemetery in the first place," he pointed out.

"And they've watched over me my entire life, but I absolutely refuse to allow them to second-guess my decisions. If they don't respect the choices I make, then they don't respect me."

He understood her stance, just as he understood the price she paid for it. "Why go to the cemetery at all? Are you sure you weren't just torturing yourself?"

"Not deliberately," she insisted, "although it might seem that way to some people. I needed to confront the past in my own way and on my own terms. I did, and I'm glad, but I'm also sorry that I've ruined our afternoon."

Michael uttered a rude word. "I couldn't care less about a few hours out of an afternoon. My only concern is that you've got the shooting in proper perspective."

"I do, Michael. Of course, I deeply regret any needless loss of life. I always will, but I can't change what happened. I did my best under very trying circumstances, and I'm committed to moving forward with my life."

"Good girl."

She laughed suddenly, her humor reemerging. "You say some of the sexist things."

Michael casually shrugged, although he felt anything but casual at that moment. He wanted Elizabeth then; he wanted her so intensely that his entire body ached. He wanted to celebrate life—her life—by making love to her. "So sue me," he challenged, his voice as inflexible as steel.

"I haven't got the free time, but thanks for the invitation. I'd much rather concentrate on a future that blends my past with the new skills I'm acquiring as I prepare to work as a psychologist. I just want what I've always wanted. I want to make a contribution to the world I live in, as idealistic as that may sound." She abruptly paused.

Michael saw the emotion welling in her eyes, but he didn't say anything. Fighting the impulse to drag her into his arms, he simply held her hand and gave her the time she needed to compose herself.

"The shooting robbed me of the joy I felt when I was a cop, and it temporarily wiped out the knowledge that I was making a difference. My former training officer saw the hell I was going through, and he gave me some excellent advice. He told me never to forget what had happened. He said if I put it completely out of my mind, I wouldn't learn from it. He made me promise to remember."

"You obviously took his advice."

Elizabeth smiled then, the first real smile he'd seen on her face that morning. Getting up from her chair, she walked to the edge of the patio and gazed out at the teal-blue Pacific. Michael followed her once he collected his crutches. Studying her posture and facial expression as he joined her, he noticed how much more relaxed she seemed. He saw why she couldn't risk trying to resurrect a career that was over. And finally, he saw the strength it had taken to confront her own limitations as a person.

She looked up at him as they stood side by side. "Thank you for helping me through this, Michael. It's been a difficult morning, but I think the worst is over now."

"You did the hard part." Unlike himself, he realized in a moment of total honesty. No matter how rigorously tested by circumstances beyond her control, Elizabeth faced down her demons.

"But only after you took on the job of emotional can opener," she reminded him quietly.

He cupped her cheek with his hand. "You look drained."

"I am, but I know what would make me feel better."

"Playing sea otter or indulging in a half marathon?"

Elizabeth shook her head. "None of the above."

"What, then?"

"Would you hold me, Michael? I need to feel connected to you right now."

Although startled, he didn't stop to think. He simply opened his arms to her. "Come here, Miss Lizzie."

Her smile nearly blinded him as she reached out to

him. He savored the sigh that escaped her as she circled his waist with her arms and tucked her face into the curve of his neck. He inhaled the scent of her. She smelled of honeysuckle roses and the sea air. She felt like heaven as she inched closer, her breasts plumping against his chest, her hips mating with his as she stood between his powerful thighs.

With nothing but heartbeats, bathing suits, and T-shirts separating them, Michael experienced a hunger in the minutes that followed that surpassed anything he'd ever felt before. His body responded to the woman nestled in his arms. His emotions, already conflicted, rioted out of control, and the restraint he'd exerted over himself since their first moments together finally snapped.

Michael took her mouth. In doing so, he did the one thing he'd vowed not to do. He staked his claim on Elizabeth.

Although he cautioned himself that he risked hurting her, his mind refused to acknowledge the warning. Michael wanted her too much to stop now. His heart paused briefly in mid-beat when he tasted Elizabeth's equally hungry response, heard her sensual moan of pleasure, and felt her fingertips dig into his lower back as she shifted closer. He considered the minutes that followed a celebration of life.

SEVEN

Elizabeth gasped when Michael's mouth settled over hers. She felt as though she'd been struck by a bolt of summer lightning. Responding to the man and his passion, she became a willing participant in her own seduction the instant she tasted his raw hunger and forbidden heat.

Molten energy rushed into her bloodstream. Common sense and caution fled her mind. She eagerly molded herself to his vital male body, inhaling each breath he released, absorbing every shudder that rumbled through his muscular frame, and then nearly weeping with relief because she no longer had to conceal the desire she felt for him.

Although somewhat dazed, she shed the lingering doubts she'd once had about making herself vulnerable to a man, but especially to this particular man, who seemed so intent on maintaining his emotional distance at all times. The walls around his heart challenged her, made her want to show him that anything was possible when two people pledged their trust and shared every imaginable intimacy. She longed to teach him that real love liberated; it didn't trap or restrain or inhibit. Real love freed. She'd seen the evidence for herself in the marriages of her parents and brothers.

Elizabeth felt more for Michael than lust or hunger, although those two sensations were a very real part of the flood of emotions threatening to swamp her. At the moment need dominated—pure, unvarnished need. It had been building momentum for weeks. Now it was like a tidal wave inside her, poised to demolish any last vestiges of resistance in its demand for total compliance.

Elizabeth nearly cried out when Michael tore his mouth from hers, but she quickly grasped his intent. Hands at his shoulders, she followed his lead when he moved backward across the patio. Several steps later he backed into the white stucco of the high wall that circled the Buckman retreat. Michael set aside his crutches, propping them against the wall on either side of his body, and reached for her.

She returned to his embrace, going up on tiptoe, wrapping her arms around his neck, her fingers tangling at his nape. She flowed against him like an unraveling bolt of the most sensual satin, sighing when she felt his arms tighten around her. His hands skimmed up and down her back, his touch possessive, incendiary. He trailed a line of scorching little kisses across her temple, along her jaw, and then down the column of her neck. She shivered, her reaction part anticipation of what was to come and part certainty that she belonged in his arms for the rest of her life.

Inhaling the blended scents of citrusy cologne and sun-warmed male, she filled her senses with his essence. The world ceased to matter. Nothing and no one beyond the perimeter of their straining bodies seemed relevant any longer. She heard him say her name. The rawness of his voice brought her gaze to his face, her heart racing when she glimpsed the emotions that filled his expression.

"I have to taste you again," he muttered.

She could only stare at him, his intensity startling her, until he leaned down and blocked out the brilliance of the midday sun once more. He took her mouth with a deliberateness that reflected his aggressive personal style, restaking his claim on her as their lips met and fused.

Their tongues mated, lazily, sensually. Elizabeth sank into the kiss. Need uncoiled within her, the kind of need that makes heat pool low in the belly before it invades every cell in the body. She felt her knees grow weak, but Michael kept her upright. She discovered that she couldn't get enough of him. She felt almost frantic, but drew solace from the fact that she wasn't alone in this feeling. Their desire took on an almost reckless quality as they feasted on each other.

Clinging to Michael, Elizabeth savored the strength she felt in his long-fingered hands as they curved over her shoulders and then trailed down her arms. A sensual image formed in her mind, an image that allowed her to visualize his hands on her naked body, exploring her at will, delving into her secrets, tantalizing her with his touch, devastating her with his thoroughness. She trembled, because she could almost feel his fingertips grazing her flesh.

Without releasing her mouth, Michael moved her, guiding her until their positions were reversed. He trapped her between the heat of his hard body and the coolness of the textured stucco, the latter penetrating the light layer of cotton covering her. The contrast of hot and cold aroused her even more, sending tremors of sensation winnowing through her slender limbs. Her breasts swelled, her nipples becoming so sensitive, they hurt. He pressed nearer still, his loins full and heavy, his musculature tightening so much so that it reminded her again of woven steel. She twisted against him, welcoming the imprint of his entire body. She felt him, felt every steely inch of his maleness. It mattered little that they were both still clothed.

Unable to control the sound, she moaned into his mouth. Her hips stirred restlessly, her insides quivered, and her pelvis tilted upward. Her nipples felt like tiny daggers of sensation, as needy as the rest of her body for greater intimacy. At that moment she would have given everything she possessed to know the feel of his mouth at her breasts.

She felt his hands suddenly tighten, the fingers spanning her waist digging into her. His throbbing body graphically conveyed his own need. Elizabeth arched into him out of instinct as another image—this time a provocative vision of their bodies merged in the ultimate sensual act—formed in her mind. She suddenly felt desperate for the knowledge of what it would be like to have him buried deeply inside her.

As though sensing the direction of her thoughts, Michael plundered her mouth. His tongue forcefully darted in and out, imitating the very intimacy she'd imagined. His teeth nipped at her lips. Elizabeth felt enflamed by his desire. She moaned his name, the sound an echo of the soul-deep desire that had been building inside her since their first moments together. That she should feel such passion for a man who shunned the idea of loving and being loved gave her pause, but only briefly.

She wanted Michael Cassidy more than she'd ever wanted a man in her entire life. Always honest with herself, Elizabeth refused to pretend there wouldn't be a price. Michael represented a very real danger, but with him she was willing to risk it all. She grasped the inevitable consequence for flawed judgment on her part. Probably a broken heart, but she accepted the reality of that or of any other as-yet-unknown penalty.

Abandoning herself to Michael's passion, she felt his hands skim up and under the loose T-shirt that covered the one-piece swimsuit she wore. She shivered in spite of the heat of the moment, his touch, and the day.

Michael drew back suddenly, peering down at her. Elizabeth shifted her hips, savoring the power of his maleness as it surged against her.

He swore, but she felt certain that the word signified the desire he felt, not anger. She touched his cheek with her fingertips, no longer able to conceal the love in her heart as she returned his gaze. She saw disbelief and shock in his hazel eyes, and she wondered then if anyone had ever truly loved him.

The look in his eyes changed abruptly. His gaze, suddenly piercing and dispassionate, swept over her. She caught her breath, saddened that he felt compelled to demonstrate that his emotions were easily controlled and that her feelings were noted and filed. His breathing gave him away though, because it suddenly wasn't quite so steady. Elizabeth knew then that she'd reached him, perhaps in a way that no one else ever had before. It hurt too much to think otherwise, just as his wariness where she was concerned hurt too.

"What?" she finally whispered, unable to withstand the silence between them any longer.

He tugged her T-shirt back into place with shaking hands before he spoke. "I cannot believe what you do to me. I ache in places I didn't even know I owned."

She smiled, her hands sliding across his broad shoulders, her fingertips massaging the muscles there. "I'm not doing anything."

He caught her hips and jerked her forward so that his powerful loins lodged in the natural cradle of her upper thighs.

Elizabeth sucked in just enough air to breathe. "Michael . . ."

"Aren't you?" he demanded, his voice roughened by desire.

She instantly capitulated. "Guilty as charged."

"I was about nineteen or twenty the last time I felt this hot for a woman."

"Hot? Now, that's an interesting word, isn't it?"

She shimmied against him, laughing low in her throat when he groaned, and his fingers dug into her hips.

"You're a tease," he accused her.

Humor sparkled in the depths of his eyes. She laughed, a rush of pure joy hitting her bloodstream like a potent drug. She challenged him, "Tell me you hate it."

"Can't stand it."

He contradicted himself when he shifted against her, back and forth, back and forth, and then a third and final time for unnecessary emphasis. They groaned in unison once he finished.

Catching her breath, Elizabeth met his gaze. "I think you're very sexy."

He arched an eyebrow.

"You look quite jaded when you do that," she teased.

The smile tugging at his lips finally triumphed over his attempt to give her a stern look. "And you look far too pleased with yourself."

"I'm just happy," she whispered.

His serious side reemerged. "I've never known anyone like you."

She felt blindsided. Cautious too. "And?"

"I don't know what to make of you."

"Michael, I'm not complicated. I'm just me."

"Then you're the only person on the planet without a hidden agenda, and you deserve an award for such selflessness."

His sarcasm stung. She tapped her fingertip against his strong chin. "Your cynicism is showing."

"So sue me."

The penetrating hazel of his eyes convinced her that he could itemize the contents of her soul at a glance. "I'd rather you kissed me again."

He demonstrated with skill and finesse just how easily arranged a kiss could be.

Breathless and shaken just moments later, Elizabeth eased backward. "I've changed my mind."

He exhaled, the sound ragged with desire. She knew then that he wanted her as much as she wanted him.

"Why?" he asked.

"It's simple."

"Then explain it to me." He leaned down, his lips at the side of her neck. "You always smell so good. Like honeysuckle roses."

"It's my soap. Do you still want to know why I've changed my mind?"

With clever lips and the tip of his tongue he continued tracing the fragrant curve that joined neck and shoulder. The kisses he left in his wake scorched like sustained bursts from a flamethrower. When she finally flattened her palms against his chest, he raised his head and peered down at her.

"Why have you changed your mind, Miss Lizzie?" he asked, obviously trying to humor her.

"I'd rather make love with you."

He looked stunned. She smiled up at him, loving his reaction.

"You're in trouble," he cautioned.

"Give me your worst," she challenged right back.

He settled against her, all hard, blatantly male flesh.

She sighed, the erotic sound issuing an invitation as old as time.

"I'd rather give you my best." He dropped a hard kiss on her lips.

A strange stillness settled over her. *Best.* There was that word. She hated it. *You're not giving the department your best when you turn tail and run.* Her ex-fiancé had used the word like a stick, beating her with it until she knew a future together would be impossible. A former marine, his law enforcement career had been his top priority. He'd expected her to feel the same way. In the end, his driven personality and his lack of compassion had forced her to walk away from their relationship.

As she looked at Michael, Elizabeth saw the confusion in his eyes. She realized that he didn't have a clue about what was going through her mind. She also realized that she loved him, loved everything about him, his physical strength, his emotional vulnerability, his sense of personal honor, his agile mind, even the control he exerted over himself.

He wanted her, but would he ever allow himself to love her? she wondered not for the first time as she exhaled heavily.

"What's wrong?" he asked.

She shook her head, then pressed her cheek against his shoulder as she circled his waist with her slender arms. Despite her attempt at self-control, she trembled.

"Talk to me, Miss Lizzie."

She suddenly felt foolish for hiding, so she relaxed within the circle of his arms and peered up at him. "I didn't know if you'd want me once I told you about last year."

His gaze narrowed. "How could any man not want you?" he asked.

"I thought . . ."

Michael shook his head. "No, you didn't. Last year was about survival and understanding your own limits as a human being, Elizabeth. It's a concept I had to come to terms with a long time ago. No one has the right to fault your judgment calls."

He was right, she realized. She hadn't thought. A gung-ho, by-the-book cop who never doubted himself, her ex-fiancé had hurt her when she'd faced the greatest crisis of her life. Her ability to trust others had been a casualty of the experience. Luckily, her self-confidence was on the upswing now.

"You've got to know by now that judging people isn't my style either."

She nodded. "I know, Michael."

"The ex-fiancé contributed to this situation, didn't he? He made you doubt yourself."

She paled but nodded, then stared at his T-shirt-covered chest.

Lifting her chin with a fingertip, he forced her to look at him. "You haven't told me everything, have you?"

She didn't bother to answer, because she knew the look on her face made it clear that she hadn't.

"Tell me now," he suggested, stopping her as she tried to extricate herself from his embrace. "Finish it, Elizabeth."

"My engagement ended the week I resigned."

"He didn't stand by you?"

"He couldn't accept my decision to resign. He, and everyone else for that matter, thought I should forget what had happened and go back to work. I couldn't. I'm not made that way."

He shook his head in disgust. "The damn fool," Michael confirmed. "He didn't have a clue about what makes you tick, did he? Remind me to send him a thank-you note."

"When things ended between us, I felt as though I didn't know him any longer. Either he'd changed, or I finally opened my eyes to the person he really was. The day after the shooting, he tried to talk me into an interview with a local investigative reporter."

"He expected you to turn a personal trauma into a media event?" he asked, his tone filled with incredulity.

She nodded. "But he did me a favor, Michael, even though it took me a while to realize it. I was already reeling from what had happened and I'd been placed on administrative leave, which was standard procedure. But I still felt betrayed and rejected when things between us fell apart. He never understood that I didn't want to be an object of curiosity."

"His loss. Forget him," Michael muttered as he swooped down once again and took her lips.

His gentleness nearly shattered her soul as he sipped at her mouth. He treated her like the finest wine, sampling her essence as he dipped his tongue between her lips, sliding past the barrier of even white teeth, tasting, taunting, and tantalizing her until she tumbled into the heated oblivion of pure sensation. She welcomed the reprieve from her memories.

Elizabeth angled her head, giving him greater access, the kind of access that makes a woman totally vulnerable to a man's passion. He explored her slowly, deliberately, and she got another taste of his remarkably sensual nature. His fingertips slid back and forth over the taut tips of her still-covered breasts. She shivered almost violently, the sensations cascading through her almost too much to bear when he closed his hands over her.

Shuddering, she arched into his touch. She felt his fingers spasm, heard the wordless sound he made. Struggling to free herself from the T-shirt she wore, she welcomed Michael's help when he pulled the shirt up and over her head. She stood before him, her gaze locked on his strained features as she peeled her bathing suit straps off her shoulders and drew the bodice away from her breasts. She let the fabric fall to her waist. Her high, full breasts sprang free, the points of her nipples a pale mauve, the rest of her skin a creamy contrast to the golden tan she'd acquired in recent days.

"Dear God," Michael said in a breathless voice.

She'd never seen such disbelief or near-reverence in a man's eyes before. She stared up at him, and all the love she felt for him spilled from her heart and rushed to her lips. She whispered his name, ready to speak the truth, but she managed at the last second not to say the words. A sigh followed, a shattered little sound that reflected the depth of her vulnerability.

"What are you thinking?" she asked.

A muscle spasmed in his clenched jaw. Stark pain showed in his eyes. "You're exquisite, Elizabeth Parker, but I don't want to love anyone. Not even you. I don't want to take that kind of a risk. I've seen the destruction that follows."

Her heart shattered into a thousand fragments as she stared up at him.

"Don't look at me like that."

"Like what?" she cried.

"As if I've just destroyed your world," he said angrily.

You have, she thought. *You've blown it straight to hell out of pure fear.*

Elizabeth wanted to scream her pain and frustration, but she smothered the wounded-animal sound echoing inside her and struggled to summon a composure she didn't feel. She twisted away from him, but he grabbed her and forced her to face him.

"Love won't hurt you," she cried. "Don't be afraid of it, or me. Please."

He stiffened, his expression thunderous as he peered at her. "I've never pretended to be someone capable of giving you what you've said you want from a man."

"And I've never asked you to give more than you're capable of giving, Michael. I wouldn't do that to you, because I know what it's like to be placed in that position."

She registered the anguish etched into his features, but his distress provided little comfort. The damage was done.

She struggled to free herself.

"Don't push me away," he whispered, his strength making a joke of her effort to put some distance between them. "Don't push me away. Let me hold you for a little while longer."

In the end, she discovered that she couldn't reject him, because his admission, not just his agonized plea, tore at the very fabric of her soul. Neither did she resist when he gathered her close, claimed her lips, and delved deeply into her mouth. She decided to stop torturing herself by wishing for the unattainable, even as she tried to come to terms with the reality of what Michael could give. She tried very hard as she lost herself in the sensations sweeping over her.

She trembled when his hands cupped her breasts. Her nipples, tight and tingling with need, nudged at the centers of his palms. He flicked his thumbs over the distended tips, then bent down to take first one, then the other, into his mouth. Streamers of scorching sensation unfurled throughout her body, and the inarticulate sounds escaping her were all she could manage as she expressed her pleasure. Feeling utterly defenseless as he tantalized her senses and branded her delicate skin, she began to prepare for complete surrender, the only option her shattered heart was willing to consider any longer.

When he straightened and took her mouth again, she slipped her hands up under his shirt. She tested the resilience of the muscles that flexed and flowed beneath her fingertips, savoring his physical strength. She wanted the kind of mating that would bridge the gaps he'd created between them and heal the wounds in his heart. She wanted to feel complete as a woman, and she knew that he was the only man capable of giving her that gift. She longed to show him, because she couldn't seem to find the right words to tell him, that sharing love was a worthy goal between two people, regardless of the unconventional start to their relationship.

"I have to touch more of you," she insisted feverishly against his lips as she tugged at the bottom of his shirt.

He responded to her words by briefly freeing himself and removing his T-shirt. "I need to feel your hands on my body," he said as he seized her wrists and brought her open palms to his chest.

His admission caught her by surprise, and it gave her hope. Michael wasn't the kind of man who used the word *need*. Not ever. She sank her fingers into the dense pelt of dark chest hair. As she caressed the hard round disks of his nipples, Elizabeth felt the powerful shudders that tore through his body. He kissed her again, his possession of her mouth so thorough that she reeled from lightheadedness when he abruptly ended their physical connection a few minutes later.

"I want you." His hard body and raspy voice made her nerve endings flutter in response.

"I want you too," Elizabeth confessed. "Make love to me, Michael. You don't need to hold back anymore. I understand your rules, and I promise to abide by them."

He groaned. She couldn't quite define the meaning of the sound, but it resonated with remorse and made her want to believe that he regretted his inability to put his emotions and his heart on the line. She wanted to believe that more than anything in the world.

Her thoughts scattered the instant he fastened his mouth to hers again. She felt as though she'd been sucked into the center of an inferno, and she stopped caring if Michael consumed or asphyxiated her with his scintillating passion. She gave herself up to the ecstasy of his hunger and his kiss, her surrender total.

"This is insane," he ground out several minutes later. Abruptly releasing her, Michael slammed his open palms against the stucco wall on either side of her head. Air raged in and out of his body.

Elizabeth sagged against the wall, breathless, shaken, and feeling as though she'd just taken a ride on the end of an out-of-control yo-yo. She looked at Michael, and the fury in his expression sent a wave of confusion washing over her. Tugging at her swimsuit with trembling fingers, she jerked the fabric over her swollen, hard-tipped breasts, then brought her hands to her face and pressed her fingertips to her pounding temples. She felt disoriented and abandoned. She didn't like those feelings; she didn't like them at all.

"We're adults, dammit, and we're acting like adolescents."

Elizabeth flinched. His words and the harshness of his voice were more than she could bear at the moment. She attempted to duck around him, but he caught her before she could move beyond his reach. Maneuvering her back against the wall, he peered down at her.

She crossed her arms over her breasts, deliberate in

her refusal to meet the gaze of the man responsible for the emotional anguish she felt. What was the point? she wondered, now thoroughly disheartened.

"I want you more than I've ever wanted a woman in my entire life, but I'm not taking you."

"That's obvious," she said, gathering up the shredded remains of her dignity.

"You're too vulnerable right now, Elizabeth."

Looking up, she glared at him, instantly furious with him. "Shall I thank you now for your nobility, or would you prefer an engraved note delivered by the postman?"

Michael swore as he shoved careless fingers through his hair, his frustration evident. Taking a steadying breath, he cupped her cheek in his hand and urged, "Don't do this. You're the last person in the world I want to hurt, but I will hurt you if we let this thing between us go any farther."

Elizabeth struggled to free herself. "Damn you, Michael Cassidy. Quit lying to yourself and to me."

"I'm not lying."

"The hell you're not. You're afraid to make love to me. You're afraid of what you might feel, not just of what you feel now."

His fingers dug into her flesh as he gripped her shoulders to hold her still. "You're wrong."

"I'm right, and we both know it." Shame and embarrassment flushed her skin. She felt thoroughly humiliated, not just angry. She didn't care about anything at that moment aside from escape. "Get your hands off me right now. I can tolerate a lot, but I won't be manipulated or manhandled, especially by you. You have a cruel streak, and I don't want any part of it."

He complied with her request, shock at her outburst evident in his expression as he shifted out of her path. Squaring her shoulders, Elizabeth pushed off the wall and marched across the wide patio. Although she wouldn't have admitted it to another soul at that moment, the right words from Michael would have stopped her in her tracks.

Unfortunately, he didn't utter a sound. She heard him grab his crutches and assumed he'd turned to watch her. She hesitated for a moment, praying that he'd say something. Anything. Still, he didn't speak. She felt his gaze on her as she collected her purse, rummaged through the contents for her sunglasses, found them, and shoved them onto her face.

Elizabeth departed the Buckman house without another word or a backward glance, anger and hurt fueling each and every step she took. She ran out of energy, though, the moment she walked into the kitchen of her own home. She slammed and locked the door, her emotions breaking free. She wept, the shattered sound an echo of her disappointment and heartbreak.

EIGHT

Elizabeth hated the pretense of trudging through the motions of daily life, but she knew she wasn't capable of anything more. She felt emotionally and physically drained after her confrontation with Michael.

In a desperate attempt to regain control of her emotions, she sought a reprieve from her disappointment by running five miles on the beach that evening. She debated every step of the way the wisdom of stopping at Seagrove Park once she completed her exercise. In the end she let her instincts guide her, and they insisted that she not hide from Michael. She mustered her dwindling courage during the final mile of her run, praying that she wouldn't fall apart if they came face-to-face.

After pulling on a sweatshirt over her unitard, Elizabeth settled in to wait for him. Darkness and low clouds that carried the heavy scent of rain enveloped the coast. A cool breeze gusted in from the Pacific, while the surf crashed against the shoreline. As she sat on the bench they'd shared every evening for several weeks, she tried to come to terms with Michael's aversion to trusting anyone with his emotions. She knew then that he'd waged a lifelong battle against any kind of emotional involvement. She also replayed in her mind what had, and had not, happened between them as she waited for him, but the sad movie offered little solace and even fewer answers.

She waited for more than an hour, but to no avail. Although she felt even more dispirited as she walked home alone that first night, Elizabeth continued to deliberately route her evening runs so that she passed by Seagrove Park. Michael remained absent, however, but not because he'd left Del Mar.

Quite the contrary, Elizabeth discovered. She caught periodic glimpses of him as the week unfolded—first at the post office, a second time standing at the deli counter at Daniel's Market when she glanced across the store from her position in the checkout line, and then seated with a group of people at the bar of the Pacifica Del Mar when she and her sister were being shown to a balcony table for lunch by the restaurant's hostess.

Elizabeth felt sick at heart every time she saw him. Michael never failed to acknowledge her presence if he noticed her, but his coolly polite nods left her both angry and stunned by his behavior. She desperately missed the welcome she'd always seen in his eyes when he'd looked at her before. She resented his attitude, although his disinterest became a remarkably effective deterrent, and saved her, she suspected, from throwing herself at him and making a complete fool of herself. Even though she considered confronting him when they encountered each other, her pride prevented her from doing it in a public place.

A part of her wanted to shake some sense into him and tell him that she was the best thing that had ever happened to him; another part of her wanted to dive beneath the covers of her bed and hide forever. Her own common sense and innate dignity prevailed, however, despite how humiliated she felt.

Although devastated by Michael's rejection, she managed not to pitch herself off the top of the nearest tall building. She made herself face each new day. She also continued to prepare for the coming semester, even though the light had gone out of her eyes and her emotions felt even more damaged than the previous year when her engagement had ended. She longed to turn to her family, but the impasse caused by the shooting prevented that option.

Elizabeth finally decided to speak to Michael, but in her own time and on her terms. Her growing anger became her catalyst, not just a part of her motivation for wanting to confront him.

From him she'd learned that in daring to love a man who didn't want to be loved, she'd risked everything— her dreams, her emotions, and her heart. Michael prompted her to seriously doubt, more now than ever before, that she would find a man capable of understanding the contradictory aspects of her own personality. Oddly enough, he'd seemed to comprehend that the sensitive, nurturing woman he'd come to know had also been a good cop. She wondered, as well, if anyone would ever grasp the ramifications of the impossible choice she'd faced in the line of duty the previous year —a choice that had tested her in ways that most people were never tested.

Michael had understood, in large part because of the difficult choices he'd faced in his life. The similarities of their individual reactions finally occurred to her as their time apart lengthened. Risk was an issue for both of them. Michael refused to risk his emotions, while she refused to risk the life of a fellow officer.

What made him unique, she eventually concluded, also made him vulnerable and inaccessible. He was, she realized in a moment of complete honesty with herself, both unable and unwilling to allow anyone access to the fragile emotions he'd learned to shield from the world. Michael was a walking contradiction—just like her in some ways, but the absolute opposite in others.

She struggled to come to terms with his rejection. It took time, but after enduring one of the loneliest weeks of her life, she felt a certain amount of relief that they hadn't become lovers. She knew in her heart that their breakup would have been even more devastating had they become intimate. Although he rarely left her thoughts, it never entered Elizabeth's mind that Michael was dealing with his own demons. She assumed that he'd made a coldly analytical choice not to proceed with their relationship.

His mood morose, Michael slouched against the couch cushions in the family room at the Buckmans', nursed a beer, and stared at the lined tablet on the coffee table in front of him. The words written on the pages concerned Elizabeth—her innate dignity, her courage, her strength of character, and all the details of the incident that had permanently changed her perception of herself and the career she'd loved. Elizabeth, the woman who made his soul ache for what would never be.

The dozen or so pages he'd penned also contained the words she hadn't been able to say aloud, the unspoken words of personal trauma and anguish—the human toll people rarely noticed in the aftermath of a tragedy. Unable to sleep, he'd committed it all to paper a few nights earlier—the facts surrounding the shooting and Elizabeth's emotions, the range and content so far-reaching, so powerful that they formed the premise for a compelling documentary.

Michael had written instinctively at first, then with even greater purpose as the events took on cinematic form in his mind. He'd worked until dawn, then spent the entire next day questioning the judgment that had prompted him to record the incident. In the end, however, he hadn't discarded his notes. He'd put his doubt and the guilt he felt on a mental back burner, aware of but unwilling to deal with the negative emotions.

Michael continued to rationalize his actions as he enhanced and edited his notes in the days that followed. He told himself that his conscience was overly active as he refined and expanded the concept emerging on paper to a workable rough draft.

A rough draft of his next documentary film.

How could it not be? he wondered.

Doubt still plagued him day and night though. His conscience kept shouting one question: Did he really intend to commit this kind of sweeping betrayal of the only woman he'd ever loved?

Michael knew in his gut that it didn't matter if the shooting was a part of the public record. Nor did it matter that Elizabeth had regained control of her life. She'd called herself a fake, but he knew the truth. The bottom-line question he had yet to answer was whether or not he would be able to live with himself if he pursued the project and opened her life up once again to the scrutiny of the media. Although fascinated by the creative possibilities, he felt torn between protecting her privacy and the potential for humanizing the men and women of the law enforcement community through a documentary that revealed the personal issues faced by every police officer in the nation.

Michael exhaled heavily. Lifting the bottle of imported beer to his lips, he downed the last of the amber-colored liquid before setting aside the empty soldier. He muttered a curse, frustrated with himself because he couldn't separate Elizabeth from his thoughts or his instincts any longer.

Falling in love with her hadn't been on his personal agenda, but it had happened. He'd fallen hard, but then he'd crashed into the reality of his past. His feelings for her, too vital to ignore but too unsettling to trust, were unlike anything he'd ever experienced with another woman. Elizabeth unnerved him, as did the hunger he felt whenever he thought about her, which was all the time now. She intrigued, she aroused, she fascinated, and she evoked hope. She also inspired genuine fear. He felt like a moth being drawn to a flame, a flame that would ultimately incinerate him. His parents had burned on the altar of love, then burned out. Their obsessive love had devastated his life. He remembered how they would cling to each other at times, declarations of undying love flowing back and forth between them; the next minute they'd be cursing each other. Michael understood the fine line between love and hate, and he knew how easily that line blurred.

He swore, the ugly word a frustration-rich hissing sound as it left his body. Getting up from the couch, he reached for the cane propped against the coffee table before he made his way to his suite of rooms. He walked into the bathroom, shed his robe, and stepped into the shower. Reaching for the soap, he worked a lather between his hands and began to wash himself, but an image of Elizabeth surfaced in his mind as he stood under the spray of hot water. A naked, smiling image that knotted his nerves and sent desire streaming recklessly through his bloodstream.

He exhaled, the sound raw. God, how he missed her. Not being with her was eating him alive, but he knew enough not to seek her out again. Spending any more time with her was too risky, even though he wanted and needed her every waking minute of the day.

Wanting, Michael understood. *Needing* was an altogether different issue.

Even though it stunned him to realize it, he needed Elizabeth. Needed her love, her passion, and her nurturing instincts in the same way that an addict needs a fix. Needed her on some soul-deep level that frustrated and terrified him. He'd vowed never to need another person, but need had become his cross to bear where she was concerned.

Needing anyone scared the hell out of Michael Cassidy. Needing reminded him of his parents, of their failed marriage, of his father's resentment when he'd realized that he had to choose between his acting career and the wife and son who needed him, and of his mother's willingness to be a victim. In his more cynical moments, Michael viewed their so-called love as nothing more than the codependence of two immature people. When he was at his most lonely, however, his mind played tricks on him and he remembered the isolated moments of happiness—happiness he still secretly craved for himself.

But Michael never let himself forget that his father's career had won in the end, his wife and young son casualties in the cutthroat game of real life. He had no intention of ever becoming a casualty again. Michael also remembered the manner in which his mother's need had been used against her. She had died needing. His parents had taught him a hard lesson—love equaled loss and abandonment. The equation was simple, and he knew better than ever to give anyone that kind of power over him. Not even a woman as unique as Elizabeth.

Once Michael finished showering, he dressed and made his way downstairs. He spotted a nattily attired Hal Buckman, the older man seated in an easy chair and sucking on one of his trademark cigars as he browsed through the handwritten pages Michael had left on the coffee table, when he walked into the sprawling combination kitchen and family room.

Michael hadn't seen Hal in more than a month, although they'd talked on the phone several times during his convalescence. His heart briefly stilled in his chest as he approached Hal, because he knew his friend would recognize the cinematic potential of Elizabeth's personal journey through hell.

"This is incredible," Hal declared as he set aside the stack of loose pages and got to his feet. "Refine it a little more, and we've got our next Oscar contender. I'll pitch it to the money men as soon as it's ready."

Despite his uneasiness, Michael casually shrugged. "Maybe. I'm not sure I want to do it, so let me think about it a little longer."

Hal walked to the coffeemaker and refilled his mug. "There's no maybe about it, son. This is first-rate material. Call the lawyers and have them option the project. We'll hire the cop as an adviser. Documentaries that show the human side of people in law enforcement are almost unheard of in this age of bleeding-heart liberals, the same liberals who keep getting bogged down with the rights of the criminal."

Michael took a seat on the couch, setting aside his

cane. He agreed in principle with Hal's evaluation of the documentary's potential, and he appreciated both his support and comprehension of the merit of the project, but he still wasn't ready to make a decision. "I'm not sure I want to pursue it. Let me think on it for a while. I need to concentrate on *Dark Side* for now."

Hal's gaze narrowed briefly. "How's the editing coming along?"

"Slow, but very steady. We wound up with more usable footage than usual. Makes it a challenge to figure out what to save and what to discard. A few more weeks, though, and I'll be ready for the sound stage."

"Good. Chuck Heston's people tell me he's willing to do the narration for us. You already know how much he likes your work, and he's got time in his schedule this fall. We need to get him on the calendar by mid-October though. Is the script shaping up?"

Grateful that Hal's focus had turned away from Elizabeth, Michael said, "I've got a rough draft. I'll be ready to turn it over to the writers fairly soon."

Their conversation continued for another hour. The two men dealt with a variety of business concerns as they shared a late lunch. Still tense about Elizabeth, Michael walked Hal to his car.

Once he was seated behind the wheel of his Mercedes, Hal commented, "I want to meet the woman cop."

"How did you know it was a woman?"

"How could it not be?" the older man asked as he applied a match to the end of a fresh Havana. "The emotional content definitely isn't male. Those guys are generally more macho than the Duke used to be, even though a lot of them are closet white knights. This is too honest. Real gut-level stuff. Has to be a woman. Is she local or someone you met in New York when you were filming *Dark Side*?"

"Local."

"Anybody I might know?"

Michael felt guilty enough already. He couldn't bring himself to lie to Hal. They'd been too close and shared too much during the course of their long friendship. "Yes, but I'd rather not say anything more about her. Privacy's an issue for her."

"All right, son. We'll talk about this another time. You're not your usual pragmatic self for some reason." His gaze became speculative as he studied Michael. "My guess is that you've finally tripped over a woman who interests you." He chuckled. "I won't say anything to Diane, though, or she'll start hearing wedding bells and make your life a living hell."

Despite his best efforts, Michael knew he failed to conceal his conflicted emotions as he spoke. "I've known a lot of interesting women, Hal."

"That isn't what I said, son." He smiled around the cigar clamped between his teeth. "Take care of yourself, and use my pager number if you need anything."

Gripping his cane, Michael stood in the driveway long after his mentor's departure. Hal read him better than most people did, and he'd never apologized to anyone for being the kind of man who spoke his mind.

Michael couldn't recall a time when he'd felt more transparent or unsettled. Everywhere he looked, he saw Elizabeth. He returned to his makeshift office and re-

sumed editing the footage for *Dark Side*, but Hal's parting remark stayed with him until he admitted to himself
that the older man was right. He hadn't been his usual
pragmatic self since meeting Elizabeth Parker, even
though he knew he couldn't allow that fact to influence
his professional decisions.

Michael's work meant everything to him. It had
given his life meaning, allowed him an outlet for his
creative ability, and had provided him with a vehicle for
success. Right or wrong, he defined himself through his
documentaries. He sensed that he always would, because he didn't know how to live any other way.

Michael attended a cocktail party two nights later.
Neighbors and friends of Hal and Diane Buckman's
had badgered him into calling a temporary halt to his
reclusiveness so that he could join them and their
guests for the evening. He finally accepted their invitation, hoping to dispel his melancholy mood.

Michael encountered several Hollywood acquain-
tances within a few minutes of his arrival, but the
person who captured and held his attention wasn't a
tinsel-town luminary or power broker extraordinaire.
He paused when he spotted Elizabeth, who stood with
a group of people—mostly men, Michael observed
sourly—on the opposite side of the glass-walled room
that fronted the Pacific.

His hungry gaze moved over her, his senses so centered on her that he saw no one else in the crowded
room. Poised and smiling, Elizabeth wore low-heeled

sandals and a short silk shift the color of ripe raspberries. Heart-shaped earrings adorned her ears, and a matching pendant suspended from a gold chain nestled in the hollow of her throat. Her dark hair, drawn away from her face in a French braid, emphasized her remarkable eyes and dramatic cheekbones. Her beauty hit him like a blow from a closed fist, and the hunger that had haunted him for days refused to remain at bay. It burst free, much like the spontaneous combustion that occurs in a forest after a long drought.

Michael lost track of time as he watched Elizabeth, the wineglass he held forgotten as he savored the sound of her laughter. He'd missed the captivating sound just as he'd missed the woman attached to it. When she glanced his way, Michael saw her smile falter and then disappear altogether. The wariness in her eyes filled him with pain and regret. He thought again about the documentary, certain now that she would interpret his use of a shared confidence as the ultimate betrayal. Michael wondered for a moment if he'd become his father.

Stunned at first when Elizabeth turned on her heel and walked to the open patio doors that led out to the beach side of the dwelling, Michael managed to jerk free of his shock just as she disappeared from sight. He followed her into the night, guided solely by instinct and desire.

She moved quickly through the darkness, her sure-footedness a reminder of her intimate knowledge of the Del Mar beach. Freed of his crutches a few days earlier, Michael gripped the curved handle of his cane and followed her at a brisk pace. He caught up with her just steps from her back door.

"Don't run from me, Miss Lizzie."

She paused, then turned slowly to face him. "Don't make the mistake of telling me what to do again, Michael. I won't tolerate that kind of high-handed behavior from you. I've gone the distance with you already, and it was a wasted effort."

He silently cursed himself when he glimpsed the distress shadowing her dark eyes, distress he knew he'd caused. Elizabeth abruptly turned away from him. She fumbled with her key before she managed to shove it into the lock.

"Elizabeth, please wait," Michael said quietly.

Her back still to him and her head bowed, she hesitated in the doorway once she pushed open the door. "Why?"

Instead of answering her, he waited for her to face him again. What could he say? he wondered. How in hell could he explain a lifetime of habits that protected him? How could he convince her that he hadn't intended to hurt her, even though he knew he had?

Elizabeth drew in a steadying breath, then squared her shoulders. She turned, meeting his gaze. She lifted her chin, the unconscious gesture a statement of defensiveness that Michael couldn't fault. She flicked a glance at his cane. "I see congratulations are in order."

He nodded, grateful for the opportunity to delay her despite the coolness of her tone. "I was ready to wrap those crutches around the nearest telephone pole."

Michael longed to reach out and touch her as they stood there. He wanted the silky smoothness of her skin and the pliability of her toned body beneath his fingertips. His gaze steady as he peered down at her, he felt hot currents of desire surge through his bloodstream, hunger for this woman as out of control as a wildfire. He wanted to bask in her scorching heat and sensuality. He wanted her even though he knew he couldn't have her. More important, he knew at that instant that he didn't deserve this woman. Instead of touching her, he closed his hands into fists.

She stared at him, emotions too diverse to label in her expressive features. Michael couldn't ignore the pain reflected in her eyes. He suddenly stepped toward her, unwilling and unable to restrain himself, although he managed not to touch her. He inhaled, filling his senses with her scent. Honeysuckle roses, a fragrance he would always connect to Elizabeth. Compelled by an acute need to have one more taste of her, he leaned down. He felt oddly disconnected from everything and everyone but Elizabeth as he watched her eyes widen with shock. The sound she made, a muffled gasp, made him pause.

"Michael . . ." she began, but then she stopped herself from saying anything more. She sidestepped him, pressing her slender body against the doorframe.

Because she looked ready to flee, Michael caught her wrist. "We need to talk."

She pulled free of him. "There's nothing left to say."

"Do you really mean that?"

"Why else would I have said it?" she asked, her temper snapping to life.

"Are you all right?"

"How dare you?" she demanded.

"I dare, because . . . because I care," he gritted out through clenched teeth.

"That's rich, really rich." She laughed, the sound hollow. "I'm fine, Michael. Just fine."

He flinched at the sarcasm in her voice. "Now convince me."

She pressed her fingertips to her forehead. "This is pointless. Why don't you go back to Los Angeles? It's obviously where you belong."

"I'm still working."

"Are you really?" she said, her disbelief obvious. "I think you're still here because you like being difficult."

"I'm working, dammit." His conscience kicked in. He amended his remark. "I'm trying to work."

"Too many distractions?" The edge in her voice contained enough contempt to cause wounds. "The beach is crowded this time of the year. Lots of fun in the sun. Hard bodies galore," she said in a tight voice as she referred to the legendary beauties who populated the California beaches.

"You're even angrier than I expected."

She inhaled sharply, then exhaled. Michael's chest hurt when he heard the sound. He recognized it for what it was—a sign of her vulnerability and grief. His mother, he suddenly realized, had sounded like that when disappointed by his father. He knew then that he *had* become his father. Stunned, he said nothing, but he couldn't help wondering about Elizabeth's reaction if he decided to go forward with the documentary based on the shooting incident that had changed her life forever.

She filled in the silence between them. "It's been a long ten days, Michael. What exactly do you want from me?"

"I've missed you."

She paled. "Don't lie."

"It's the truth."

"I don't think you're capable of the truth, at least not where we're concerned. You're too busy hiding your feelings so that you don't have to take any risks. You haven't called, Michael. You haven't stopped by my cottage, and you haven't been to the park. The three times you noticed me last week, you nodded and then turned away. That's not my idea of missing someone."

"Dammit, Elizabeth, what do you want from me?" he exploded, feeling cornered.

"I don't want anything." She half turned, her intent obvious.

He reached out. He grazed her shoulder with his fingertips, then watched in horror as she recoiled from his touch.

"Don't. I can't bear it right now."

"I did what was best for us. If I hadn't—"

She cut him off. "I didn't believe you the first time, and I still don't, so quit lying to me and to yourself."

"I owe you an explanation," he remarked, determined to reach her.

"What you owe me is an apology," she said.

"You've been cruel, and I haven't earned that kind of treatment from you."

"I'm not going to disagree with you."

"You wanted me, Michael, and I wanted you. Nothing could have been simpler, regardless of the day I'd had, but you turned me away."

"I didn't want to use you."

"I told you I understood your rules, and I was willing to abide by them. Why wasn't that good enough?"

"You deserve better than me."

She laughed bitterly. "So you were doing me a favor? Saving me from myself because I was showing poor judgment?"

"Dammit . . ."

"Quit swearing at me. Talk to me. Tell me the truth. Say the words out loud. There isn't a woman on this planet you'd trust with your emotions. You don't trust anyone."

"You're wrong," he automatically insisted.

"Am I?" She shook her head. "I don't think so."

"You couldn't be more wrong. I trust you. I just don't trust myself."

She gave him a skeptical look. "You didn't think I could handle an affair? Do you really expect me to believe that?"

He set aside his cane and placed his hands against her upper arms. She didn't try to move beyond his reach, and relief filled him. The wary look on her face didn't depart. Running his palms up and down the smooth, warm surface of her skin, he saw the pain and confusion in her eyes. He'd put her through hell by trying to keep her out of the hell that was his soul.

"You wanted me. So please tell me why you suddenly stopped wanting me."

"I haven't stopped wanting you," he confessed, his hands tightening on her. "I probably never will. Try to understand that what happened to us has everything to do with me and the choices I made a long time ago. I won't live my life needing anyone. Need destroys."

"Only when it's misunderstood or used against a person!" she exclaimed.

"You don't understand."

"Then help me to understand, because I'm having a very difficult time with your rejection."

"The last thing I wanted to do was hurt you."

Tears brimmed in her eyes, but she blinked them back. "But you did."

And I will again if I do the documentary. Shifting his gaze, he peered up at the moon and worked at controlling his tumultuous emotions. A brilliant sphere of bright white, it hung in the black night sky like an electrified ball. As he stood there, Michael searched for the right words. He finally spoke, but what he said sounded inadequate even to him. "I've told you about my family. The experience taught me to stay uninvolved."

"That's crazy, Michael. You can't go through life pretending your emotions aren't relevant. Everyone deserves to love and be loved. Everyone. Even you."

He stiffened. He'd heard those words before, but never from someone who mattered to him—someone like Elizabeth. Returning his gaze to her upturned face, he said, "I've done fine until now."

"You're lying to yourself again," she accused him.

His temper unraveled even more. "Quit with the blasted Pollyanna routine! You aren't a fool. I know what I saw, and I know what happens to people who need too much."

"You're not your parents, but you've managed to convince yourself that you aren't capable of a healthy relationship because they didn't have one. When someone comes along and makes you feel, you sabotage the relationship. How many times have you done this to yourself? How many, Michael?"

"I won't be like them!" he insisted.

She stared at him. "But you are becoming like them, and you don't even realize it. They were crippled. So are you if you won't let yourself feel. Do you honestly believe that by not needing anyone and by not feeling an emotion like love, you'll save yourself from heartache?"

"I'm not like them," he said stubbornly. "I'll never be like them. They were love addicts, sucking all the life and the hope out of each other until nothing was left."

"Then why are you standing here talking to me? Why do you look as though you've been to hell and back since we were last together? Your past is the key to your future, but if you don't deal with it, if you refuse to find resolution by burying your ghosts once and for all, you'll never be free to be happy."

"I told you once, I don't need a shrink."

"My God, Michael. You're an intelligent man, and you know that counseling isn't a sign of weakness. It's a sign of courage."

"Forget it."

She exhaled in frustration. "Oh, Michael, I feel sorry for you, because you're kidding yourself."

"Don't," he said, his voice rapier sharp.

"Why shouldn't I feel sorry for you?" she demanded.

"I don't want your pity."

He knew he had it, though, when he saw the look in her eyes. He knew, too, that she would eventually feel more than pity. She would hate him once she learned of the documentary.

Elizabeth paused, then faced him squarely. "You don't want anything or anyone, do you? You've barricaded your heart and flipped some internal switch on your feelings. You're out there in the world by yourself. Mr. Lone Stranger. No one to trust. No one to love. No one to share the triumphs or the failures. Enjoy yourself, Michael. It sounds like a marvelous way to live."

Her fury and sarcasm rang in his ears as she turned away from him. He moved quickly, following her into the dimly lit kitchen and anchoring her in place when he seized her hands. Her gaze flew to his face, and he felt gut-punched when he saw the tears sparkling like diamonds on her eyelashes, tears he'd caused.

"Don't turn your back on me," he said. His voice sounded like a long stretch of gravel road.

"You're a smart man, Michael Cassidy, but this is a

supremely stupid way to live. It's also unnecessary. You break my heart. You absolutely break my heart."

Her tears spilled free. He muttered a coarse word as he drew her against his body. She struggled, but he couldn't bring himself to release her. An inarticulate sound of frustration escaped her. Slumping against him, she stopped fighting and wept as he held her.

"Please don't cry." He felt like a hunted animal, desperate to protect himself but unable to stop thinking about what he was losing in his quest to safeguard his emotions. "Please."

Elizabeth finally lifted her head from his shoulder. When she began to ease free, Michael reluctantly let her go. He lowered his hands to his sides and watched her wipe away her tears with her fingertips.

"I pity you, Michael. No, I pity both of us. Your heart is paralyzed, because you insist on clinging to the past. You're denying yourself happiness out of fear. If you ever expect to know any real joy in your life, you're going to have to choose between remaining a cripple and really living. Your past is like a curse, but only because you refuse to use it the right way. It doesn't matter that I've fallen in love with you, because you can't bring yourself to trust what I feel for you or the foundation we've already begun to build. For your own sake, learn from what your parents did to each other. Be smarter than they were, because you're behaving as unwisely as they once did. Be better than the man you call your father," she challenged. "Life is filled with tough choices. I know, because I've had to make them and then live with the results. Now it's your turn. Stop with this existence you call living. Life, whether good or bad, is meant to be experienced, not watched from a distance."

She straightened her shoulders, and her chin rose a fraction of an inch. As he grappled with her unexpected admission that she loved him, not simply her challenge that he become a better man than his father, Michael reeled from this sampling of Elizabeth's courage. He wanted to believe that his life could be different. He desperately wanted to believe that love didn't wreak havoc, but doubt plagued him.

"You've become your father, even though you didn't intend that to happen. He turned his son into a bitter man. What a sad legacy."

He opened his mouth to speak, then snapped it shut. What could he say in his own defense? Was she right? How in God's name had he become the man he'd loved and hated as a child?

"I'm sorry. I had no right to say that."

"You have a right to your opinion," he gritted out, trying to come to terms with the fact that despite her pain, Elizabeth had risked her heart and her pride to fight for his emotional survival. No one had ever done that for him before. No one.

Michael knew he had to speak as they stood there. It was his last chance. As he gazed down at her, he found the strength to utter three simple but profoundly complicated words, words that made him feel more vulnerable than he'd ever felt in his entire life, words that tore his insides apart even as he said them. "I need you."

She froze. "What did you just say?"

"I need you."

"Why . . . now?"

"I'm not sure," he admitted, although he was. He couldn't lose her, even if he wound up destroying them both.

She lifted her fingertips to her temples as she peered at him.

"Headache?" he asked, almost grateful for the distraction.

She lowered her hands. "No. Shock, I think."

"Don't feel alone." He felt uncertain, and didn't try to conceal it for a change.

"Where do we go from here?"

"I need to hold you," he said.

She glided closer. Michael reached out for her, silently thanking God that he hadn't completely alienated her. He gathered her against his chest, a ragged sigh escaping him. "I also need to make love to you. Will you have me?"

She smiled tremulously at him. "You're definitely getting the hang of that word, aren't you?"

He looked at her, his expression stark. "I think I need the practice."

"No pun intended?"

"No pun intended." Leaning down, he shifted his attention to lips that reminded him of ripe fruit.

She ducked, and his kiss landed on her cheek. "Is this your idea of an apology?"

He groaned. "Don't torture me. And yes, it is if you'll accept it."

"I accept, but only because I've lost my mind."

"Maybe we both have," he muttered a heartbeat before he anchored her head between his broad palms.

He kissed her then. She tasted of sweetness and compassion and desire, everything he'd ever imagined love would taste like. He couldn't get enough of her, his hunger for her voracious as he deepened their kiss by slanting his mouth across her lips. He drank from her, nourishing his heart with the flavors and textures of her mouth, replenishing his soul with the seemingly endless depths of her understanding of the demons he faced. That she was willing to fight for him still astounded him. That she could love him amazed him. Would she fight for him or would she hate him when she learned the whole truth? he wondered.

Elizabeth moaned into his mouth, the sound coming from deep inside of her and banishing his last thought. Curling into him, she fumbled with the buttons of his shirt.

Michael stayed her hands. They would talk later, he silently promised himself as he swung her up against his chest. He would tell her what he wanted to do with her story. For now, though, he allowed himself to be selfish. He needed her, needed to sink into her flesh and lose himself in the cleansing fire of her passion. Michael Cassidy needed now, just as he needed to forget his past and the future.

Her slender arms circled his neck. Her fingertips kneaded his nape. Her touch set his body on fire as he carried her out of the kitchen and into the hallway, his limp barely perceptible. He tore his mouth free, but only long enough to ask, "Which way?"

"Second door on the right," she whispered against his lips.

Michael knew then that he would never get enough of her, although he had every intention of trying. The need he felt still unnerved him, but he wouldn't, *couldn't*, deny himself any longer. He just prayed that Elizabeth was as strong as he believed her to be— strong enough to teach him how to love and strong enough to forgive him if he decided to do the documentary.

NINE

They stood face-to-face beside her bed, their eyes locked on each other as they shed their clothing. The soft glow of a bedside lamp provided illumination in a bedroom painted a pale rose. A darker rose quilt and sham-covered pillows at the top of the bed invited a closer inspection and promised comfort. The white shutters on the windows, closed now, assured privacy.

Still somewhat fearful that Michael might pull back, Elizabeth paused in the act of peeling her shift down over her breasts. Sensing that this time was different, she took a steadying breath, consciously willing herself to move beyond her own lingering anxieties. She loved him. Nothing else mattered at the moment.

The strapless, mauve lace bra she wore emphasized the bounty of her high breasts and enhanced the beauty of her flawless skin. The approval she glimpsed in his eyes made her breathing grow even choppier than it already was, and her fingers shook as she fumbled with the fabric already pooled at her waist.

Never taking his eyes off her, Michael kicked aside his shoes, stripped off his shirt, and then stepped out of his trousers. Straightening, he tossed the last two items onto a nearby chair. Clad only in a pair of dark briefs, the fabric revealed his potent maleness.

Elizabeth stared at him. She couldn't help herself, although she'd seen him numerous times in shorts and T-shirts and knew the power of his muscular anatomy. This was different. Private. The ultimate intimacy between two people. The world ceased to exist.

Michael was everything she'd ever dreamed of, the perfect mate. Toned and tanned, his body invited her touch. She met his gaze again, the heat in his eyes as he peered back at her freezing the air in her lungs. She knew she'd never seen that kind of intense desire in the eyes of any other man who'd looked at her.

He reached out to her, stopping her when she began to complete the process of removing her dress. "Let me."

She let him, a shattered little sigh escaping her as he tucked his fingers beneath the fabric of her shift and slid it past her hips. Bending over her as he eased her dress free of her body, his fingers and palms skimmed down the length of her legs to her ankles, his lips whispered across her shoulder and then anointed the sensitive skin of her neck. She trembled, so sensitized by his touch that she felt almost faint. Her dress puddled at her feet, the raspberry silk forgotten the instant she stepped out of it.

Michael made her feel utterly feminine as he embraced her. His manhood, a hard ridge of desire, pressed against her lower abdomen and sent a glittering array of sensations into her bloodstream.

She felt fragile, yet also strong, vulnerable, yet very certain that what they were about to share was right. She shimmied closer, his possessive embrace and the groan that escaped him empowering her to reveal her feelings. "I want you so much, Michael."

"I've never known anyone like you," he said, his voice hoarse as he took her lips.

His claiming was the tenderest thing she'd ever experienced in her entire life. Moved by his gentleness, she almost wept. This was what she'd waited for, hoped for, and prayed for. He wanted her enough to trust her with his emotions, and that knowledge made her heart soar even as she ignored the voice in her head that asked—*but for how long?*

His hands at her back as he tenderly kissed her, he freed the clasp that held her bra in place and tugged it away from her body. It landed on the floor, joining the discarded raspberry silk shift. He cupped her breasts. She gasped, and he took the sound of surprised pleasure into his mouth, sipping from her lips, worshipping her with his tongue and hands and fingertips, tantalizing her, silently but eloquently promising her the fulfillment of every fantasy she'd ever had as he fanned the flames of her desire.

She touched him, too, her open palms sliding up and down his back. She traced the line of his spine down to the elastic waistband of his briefs with her fingertips, then went lower still, her hands traveling beneath the stretchy fabric to his firm buttocks. When she cupped them, he jerked in response to her sensual touch, his manhood throbbing against her belly, his breathing becoming so ragged that he wrenched his mouth free and threw his head back to catch his breath. She looked up at him, saw the strain in his hard-featured face, the near grimace of his lips. His eyes fell closed, the dark auburn lashes as thick as mink as they shadowed his high cheekbones.

"My God," he rasped out. "What you do to me is beyond anything I've ever felt before."

"Michael . . ." she began to say, wanting to express the fullness of her heart, but he silenced her with his lips, this time with a force that enflamed her senses.

He guided her toward the bed, shoving aside the pillows and stripping back the quilt without relinquishing her mouth. They tumbled across the sheet-covered mattress together, landing on their sides, mouth to mouth, chest to breasts, thigh to thigh. Elizabeth's hands skimmed over him. She explored him at will, enjoying her freedom.

Michael eventually eased her onto her back, his hands closing over her breasts as he repositioned himself in a crouch over her, his legs bent at the knees and bracketing her thighs. Fingering her nipples, he watched them tighten into snug rosebuds. Elizabeth moaned, her eyes falling closed. No man had ever made her feel more desired or more proud to be a woman than she felt now.

Time ceased to matter as he extended his tender

torment. Tugging at her nipples, he aroused her until she almost begged for his mouth. She didn't speak, though, because she didn't want to rush what they were sharing. She wanted to feel every possible sensation, every possible emotion.

"Talk to me," he urged. "Tell me what you're feeling."

She smiled, a slow, scintillating smile that would have scorched a lesser man. "Everything," she whispered in response to his quiet command, her husky voice never more distinctive or seductive.

Michael settled more firmly against her, the fullness of his loins nudging the top of her thighs. She shivered, then arched up, her body issuing an instinctive invitation to the man she loved. Opening her eyes, she saw the strain he was under etched into his features. He filled his lungs with oxygen, then exhaled raggedly before he bent down and captured a nipple between his teeth.

Elizabeth gasped. She gripped his shoulders, sensation after sensation coursing through her. Michael sucked more forcefully, drawing the taut bud deep into his mouth and swirling the tip of his tongue over it. She began to chant his name, the sensual sound repeatedly spilling past her lips. He shifted to her other breast several minutes later, devastating her senses all over again. She was breathless when he finally lifted his head and peered at her, a satisfied smile on his face.

"You're trying to make me crazy," she accused him weakly.

"You don't like?" he teased. He trailed his fingers

over her distended nipples, smoothed them back and forth across the underside of her breasts, then dragged them down over her quivering belly.

"I like." She gasped as sensation overtook her yet again. "I like very much."

She trembled under his clever hands as he continued his quest to arouse her, but she also initiated an erotic mission of her own when she placed her hands on his powerful thighs. Kneading his muscles, she slowly worked her way to his groin, her fingertips unerring as they found his hardness. She watched his face the entire time she fondled him, her delight apparent when an agonized groan burst past his gritted teeth. The fabric covering his maleness was nothing more than a minor impediment, but she wanted it gone.

"I'm naked," she observed.

"I know," he muttered, his fingertips combing through the silk at the top of her thighs.

"I don't want to be the only one."

He smiled at her, as though he'd simply been waiting for an invitation. "That can be arranged." He slipped to one side of her, shed the garment, and rejoined her. This time, though, he stretched out atop her, his hips lodging between her parting thighs, his arms bracing his weight so that he wouldn't crush her.

She arched upward. He made a delicious sound, a low groan of raw hunger that did amazing things for her confidence.

"Your wish is my command, Miss Lizzie."

"I want you inside of me."

His eyes flared wide with surprise, but Michael

shook his head. "As tempting as that sounds, it's too soon."

"Too soon?" she said, her gaze hungrily skimming over his angular facial features, her hands at the base of his spine, fingers kneading, palms pressing rhythmically. She shifted seductively beneath him, and he bit back yet another groan. "Doesn't feel too soon to me."

"Trust me," he urged, his voice ragged.

"I do," she whispered.

His frown was brief, but she noticed it. Although disconcerting, she didn't have time to question it, because Michael was already in motion. Coherent thought quickly became impossible. She cooperated as he guided her into a reclining position against a grouping of pillows at the head of the bed.

"Relax, Elizabeth."

She uttered an inarticulate sound of assent and tried to do as he suggested.

He bracketed her hips with his hands. His warm breath washed over her delicate flesh an instant before she felt the first flick of his tongue. Elizabeth gasped, the sound a blending of shock and pleasure. He covered her with his mouth, sampling her essence and delving deeply into the heart of her desire with a thoroughness that left her reeling and pliable beneath his skillful hands and mobile mouth.

Tension gathered low in her belly. Michael seemed intent on consuming her with his sensuality, but she didn't fear his power over her. She savored it, just as she cherished his desire to possess her so intimately. She undulated against him, her pelvis tilting upward, her nerve endings fluttering madly just beneath the surface of her skin, and her femininity becoming swollen and slick with the heavy dew of her desire.

Michael penetrated her with his fingers, his tongue simultaneously flicking back and forth across the tight knot of sensitive flesh that throbbed in tandem with her heartbeat. She writhed under his hands and mouth, her body's craving for completion more urgent with each passing second. He intensified his assault on her. She surged up from the pillows, clutching at his shoulders and brokenly whispering his name.

Elizabeth suddenly jerked under his hands and mouth, then moaned, the low sound escalating in pitch as he vaulted her into the heavens. She screamed his name as she came completely apart, the force and power of her climax so overwhelming that she felt sucked into a tumult that threatened her very sanity. She didn't want the feeling to ever end.

Michael was unrelenting. He plied his magic, thrilling her, devastating her, very nearly ruthless in his determination to sustain the peak of her climax for as long as he could. She finally collapsed in a boneless slump against the pillows. He held her afterward, clasping her close as she floated in the aftermath of the shattering experience he'd just given her, his cheek resting on her upper thigh, his hands gentle as he soothed her with the circular motion of his fingertips.

Elizabeth lost touch with reality. Her consciousness centered on Michael and the pleasure still rippling through her body. Anything and anyone else were irrelevant to her. She felt treasured and cherished for the first time in her life.

Michael moved up her still-trembling body, his hands traveling deftly over the taut skin of her stomach, his lips following the same path. He left a trail of hot, open-mouthed kisses that stimulated her senses, surprising her because until a moment before, she'd thought she might never be able to move again. When she felt him gently teethe one of her nipples, she opened her eyes.

He met her gaze, his smile more tender than anything she'd ever seen. Palming her breasts, he planted a hard kiss on her mouth. "Hi there."

She gave him a look that reflected just how thoroughly stunned she was by his sensual generosity. "Hi there yourself," she whispered in a dazed little voice.

"You're something else, Miss Lizzie."

"I didn't do anything."

"That's what you think."

Gathering her against his chest, he rolled onto his back. She wound up sprawled across him, and she immediately felt the strength of his desire.

"It's my turn," she promptly said. Sliding off him and onto her knees at his side, she peered at him through half-lowered lashes. She reached out, gently smoothing her fingertips across his cheek. When he clasped her hand and pressed a kiss to the tips of her fingers, she smiled.

"You look like a cat with a full dish of cream," he remarked.

"Do I?" She grinned, scanning his reclining body. "Shall I purr for you?"

He tensed under the sweep of her heated gaze. "I don't know if I'd survive the experience. I'm in big trouble, aren't I?"

She laughed softly, seductively, then traced the length of his torso, her fingertips gliding through the wedge-shaped pelt of dark hair that covered his muscular chest, arrowed down his flat belly, and then gathered in a nest around his manhood. "I guess that remains to be seen," she said, finally answering him as she met his gaze.

He shuddered under her erotic touch, but he didn't say anything. He simply trusted her.

"Feel good?" she asked as she nuzzled his throat with her lips and grazed his body with her fingertips.

"Better than good."

"This is just the beginning."

"But it may be the end of me."

"I have every confidence that you'll hold up under the pressure."

"Pressure being the operative word," he gritted out as she leaned down.

She smiled against his lips, then kissed him, a long, slow, hot kiss meant to devastate. She tasted both Michael and the lingering essence of her own arousal as she tangled her tongue with his, and the combination of flavors hit her senses like an aphrodisiac. She delved even more deeply, then sucked his tongue into her own mouth, her appetite for him evident as she expressed her emotions and her passion for him.

She felt his hand curve over the back of her head. When he drove his fingers into her dense hair, he flexed the tips against her scalp. She grasped the possessiveness in that simple gesture, and she took it into her heart and savored it. Her breasts swayed against his shoulder as she bent over him, her nipples tightening into aching points of sensation the instant they came into contact with his hot skin. Deep in the pit of her stomach Elizabeth felt her insides begin to clench in anticipation.

She freed his mouth, pressed a light kiss against his chin, another at the base of his throat, and yet another on his shoulder. She unraveled slowly, flowing over him, her mouth avid as she pressed kisses to his chest, pausing twice to draw his hard nipples into her mouth and suck on them until he groaned and shuddered. Her fingers simultaneously roamed over him. She touched him everywhere, and then she kissed every spot she touched, intent on creating a tension in Michael that matched the tension already threatening to spiral wildly out of control within the confines of her own body.

Dedicated solely to his pleasure, she moved lower still, her tongue darting out to paint his muscle-ridged belly with invisible strokes of wet heat. She physically expressed her love, but she didn't forget that Michael still needed to free his heart from the shadows of the past in order to love and be loved. Combing her fingertips through the coarse hair that surrounded his aroused manhood, she bent down to caress him with her lips and tongue. He jerked beneath her, his hands fisting in the bedcovers as he moaned her name.

She gave him everything she had to give with a sensuality that reflected the depth of her erotic nature. Guided by instinct, she bathed him in the healing fire of her passion. Her heart overflowed with love for him, her desire to tantalize and please the sole motivator of her actions. She took her time, deliberately and repeatedly pushing Michael to the edge of his tolerance, until she pushed him one too many times.

He surged up from the bed, a hoarse cry torn from his lips as he seized her and tumbled her onto her back. He wound up atop her, the strain of her sensual torture evident in his taut expression and even tauter anatomy. Despite his need, he took the time to reach for his trousers, but Elizabeth brought her hands to his shoulders and stopped him.

She answered the question she saw in his eyes. "We don't need barriers. I'm on the pill, and my health is excellent."

His hand trembled as he ran his knuckles along the curve of her jaw. "You're safe with me, Elizabeth. I wouldn't ever jeopardize you."

She understood his meaning, but she knew that he was also making a statement about his feelings for her. Her heart swelled with emotion, and she didn't let herself dwell on the words she really wanted to hear from him. She loved enough for both of them right now. She accepted Michael on his terms, urging him closer.

Elizabeth felt the searing heat and the power of his loins as he positioned himself between her thighs. Gripping his hips, she undulated beneath him, her body begging for his penetration while she welcomed his ravenous kisses. He surged into her without warning, settling deeply inside her in one smooth motion. She gasped, and tears pooled in her eyes—tears of relief because the waiting was finally over.

He took her on a journey to completion that exceeded every fantasy she'd ever had about lovemaking. Nothing she'd experienced in her life had prepared her for the intimacy they now shared. That realization was Elizabeth's last conscious thought as she surrendered to Michael's sensuality. Her body became the instrument and the voice of her feelings for him. He dominated her universe, each deep penetration of her body binding her to him for all eternity. She knew then that she would love him forever.

He quickened his pace as she clung to him. They stared at each other, gazes locked, bodies joined together as they sought fruition. It happened suddenly. Elizabeth moaned low in her throat as she frantically surged against him. Michael reacted with quick, sharp thrusts that sent shock waves all the way to her soul.

Elizabeth gasped Michael's name as her release claimed her. Undone by the stunning intensity of her climax, he lost control. He plunged deeply into her, giving in to the milking sensations of her body. She writhed beneath him, a captive of the climax quaking through her even as she triggered his release. He came with a strangled-sounding shout, his life force jetting hotly into her. Finally collapsing atop her, Michael buried his face in the curve of her shoulder, his chest heaving as he struggled for air.

Sprawled beneath the comforting weight of his

body, Elizabeth felt periodic aftershocks tremor through her, but she welcomed them as a reminder of the unbridled passion they'd just shared.

His respiration uneven, Michael shifted their still-joined bodies to one side a short while later. Elizabeth burrowed against him, sleepily murmuring her love as she looped her arms around his neck. A contented sigh escaping her, she closed her eyes and drifted off.

He held her as she slept, his conscience giving him no peace. His desire to use her experience as a police officer as the basis for a documentary still warred with his feelings for her. Aware of the potential damage to Elizabeth, he questioned whether or not he would be able to move forward with the project despite its potential for success. She meant the world to him, and he felt obliged to show her the rough outline of the documentary he wanted to do. He owed her that much, he knew.

Michael roused Elizabeth to feverish passion throughout the night, each interlude healing his damaged soul a little more. He was relieved that she didn't seem to notice his unexpressed worry or the desperate quality of his touch. Michael Cassidy felt certain that this would be their only night together once Elizabeth read the proposed documentary.

TEN

Michael announced his need for sustenance well before dawn. Elizabeth echoed his sentiments, noting that they'd missed the hors d'oeuvres they'd been invited to enjoy at the cocktail party the previous evening.

Hand in hand, they adjourned to the kitchen, where they inspected the contents of the pantry and refrigerator.

She began to assemble ingredients on the kitchen counter. Michael assisted. At least, he said he was assisting. He caressed her whenever she stepped within reach, then pointed out that she didn't seem inclined to dodge his hands or mouth. He repeatedly impeded her culinary efforts, but she forgave him when he confessed that he couldn't resist her naked form. Her own hands were just as curious, especially since he was equally naked, but only until their stomachs growled loudly and in unison during a deep, searching kiss. Startled by the sound, they collapsed against each other, howling with laughter.

They shared the meal preparations in earnest after that. Once she turned on the burners beneath two frying pans, one filled with eggs to be scrambled, the other lined with bacon, Elizabeth wryly remarked that playing slap and tickle was fun, but only an unwise man expected a woman to fry anything at a hot stove while attired in her birthday suit.

Glancing at her exposed assets, Michael recognized the potential for disaster and went in search of her bathrobe and his trousers.

Thirty minutes later they departed the kitchen. Michael stepped out onto the rear patio of the cottage, balancing a tray piled high with silverware, napkins, place mats, a jar of homemade strawberry jam, two mugs, and a full coffee thermos. His destination was the table positioned in the center of the gazebo. Surrounded by climbing roses and sumptuous ferns, the modest structure guaranteed both privacy and a view of the Pacific all the way to the horizon.

Elizabeth followed just moments later, carrying two plates that contained generous servings of scrambled eggs, crisp slices of bacon, grapefruit halves, and buttered triangles of toast. As they sat facing each other across the table for two, they indulged their appetites for good food, relaxed conversation, and shared laughter.

Michael couldn't help his smile as he watched Elizabeth dig into her breakfast. She was a woman with a healthy appreciation for food, and she made no apologies for it. Because she burned up more calories than most people as a result of her daily exercise regimen, she knew better than to stint on proper nutrition.

He realized not for the first time that he'd never known anyone quite like her. Honest, accessible, instinctive in her ability to love, she'd made him feel welcome in every aspect of her life. Michael still found it hard to believe that she was willing to love him and accept him on his terms. He found it even harder to believe that he'd admitted his need to her, but he had despite the fact that he hadn't uttered those words to another soul—not even Hal Buckman, his mentor and friend—since childhood. No one had ever inspired the kind of emotional trust necessary for such an admission from him; at least, no one had inspired him to try until Elizabeth.

His trust, however, wasn't complete. Michael couldn't completely surrender a lifetime habit of self-preservation after only one night in the arms of a woman, not even a woman he loved.

His guilt gnawed at him as well. He wanted to tell Elizabeth about the documentary, but he couldn't seem to find the words or the courage. Michael had never viewed himself as a coward, but he felt like one now as he made a deal with his conscience to delay the revelation. He needed everything she offered, and the years of emotional deprivation he'd endured helped him to rationalize the choice he now made. He told himself that her reaction would be the same—outright rejection —whether he told her now or if he waited a few days.

The man with the fist-size hole in his soul opted to wait.

"Penny," she said, her smile tender as she looked at him, her shapely body concealed from view by the voluminous, floor-length terry robe she wore. With her tousled locks, kiss-swollen lips, soulful eyes, and that sultry voice, she personified the classic male fantasy of the perfect woman to face across the breakfast table.

Summoning a smile, Michael firmly cast aside his worrisome thoughts. The truth would be told soon enough. "You'll have to up the ante. I don't come quite that cheap." As he spoke, he recalled the way in which she'd repeatedly astounded and delighted him throughout the night. Smart, funny, passionate, tender-hearted, and innately sensual, she'd captured his heart and captivated his senses.

"Fifty cents," she offered before taking a bite of toast.

He shook his head. "No sale. You'll have to go higher."

The emotions she aroused and yearnings she inspired still unnerved him. A risk taker all his life, Michael knew the jeopardy he now faced had catastrophic ramifications, but he couldn't help himself. He couldn't stay away from her, although he understood that the time he spent with Elizabeth undermined the emotional safety zone he'd created for himself.

Neither could he dismiss her or her admission of love. Emotional starvation did that to a man, he decided. He knew she really loved him, loved him with such honesty and sincerity that he felt humbled and undeserving—but wary too, more wary than he'd felt in years, despite the surface calm he exhibited.

"Eighty-five cents. That's all the change in my piggy bank." She filled her fork with the last of her scrambled eggs and brought them to her mouth, her eyes sparkling with laughter as she looked at him.

"Sold, but only if you throw in what's left of your bacon and that slice of toast you've been hoarding for the last fifteen minutes."

Setting aside her fork, she stacked the bacon slices on the triangle of toast and handed them over. "I'm stuffed anyway." As soon as he sank his teeth into the bacon she'd just surrendered, she cautioned, "There's a price tag attached to my generosity."

Michael finished the bacon, then drained the coffee from his mug. "The dishes?"

She shook her head, smiling as she set aside her napkin, got to her feet, and walked around to his side of the table. Straddling his powerful thighs as she would a saddle, she made herself comfortable atop him, her robe settling around their lower bodies like a tent. She leaned forward, planted a quick kiss on his lips, and then looped her arms around his neck. "You, sir, get to wash my back."

"Agreed, but only if I get to watch you wash everything else first."

Elizabeth grinned. "You're more than welcome to assist during the entire procedure, if you feel so inclined."

"I'm definitely inclined."

He grasped her chin and guided her closer. After

licking away the smudge of jam at the corner of her mouth, he covered her lips and darted his tongue into the recesses of her mouth, savoring the unique flavors of this most incredible woman. Life without her, he realized, would be a barren wasteland.

Elizabeth moaned. Angling her head to the side, she deepened their contact even more. Michael sucked at her tongue, drawing it partially into his mouth. He felt her clutch at his shoulders, her fingernails scoring his flesh. When he released her lips, they were both breathless.

"You still haven't told me what you were thinking about before," she reminded him when she could speak.

He couldn't bring himself to do it, so he side-stepped the real truth. "I was thinking about what it feels like to be inside you."

She moaned softly as she eased back in the circle of his arms, her gaze fixed on his facial features. "Are you going to tell me?" she asked, her voice husky.

"I'd rather show you."

She shivered.

"Cold?"

She shook her head.

"What, then?"

"Hot," she whispered, her eyes flaring wide as he caressed her with his heated gaze. "Very, very hot."

Because their position in the gazebo assured them of total privacy from anyone on the beach or in a neighboring dwelling, Michael didn't hesitate to tug free the belt of her robe and peel apart the lapels of the garment. Smoothing his hands over the tops of her parted thighs, he slipped them under her knees and lifted her legs. Once he finished, her knees were bent and her bare feet rested on either side of his hips. He then drew her robe around their bodies like a cape without obscuring his view of her.

Exposed to Michael's gaze, Elizabeth held perfectly still. The only sign of her vulnerability was the pulse fluttering wildly in the hollow of her throat. When he saw it, Michael leaned forward and laved the spot with the tip of his tongue.

She trembled like a willow subjected to the faintest breeze. He watched her skin flush to a pale shade of rose as he combed his fingers through the silken tangle at the juncture of her thighs, skimmed his knuckles over the enticing curve of her belly, and then moved up her midriff to her high breasts. He cupped them, the weight of the hard-nippled globes and the silky smoothness of her skin arousing him almost to the point of pain. Yet again, he couldn't get enough of her.

Elizabeth didn't make a sound. Neither did she breathe for several moments.

He smiled indulgently. "Take a breath before you faint on me." He palmed her breasts and slid his thumbs back and forth across her distended nipples. "Your body wants mine."

She smiled, an evocative smile that very nearly seared his soul as she reached down and caressed him through the fabric of his trousers. Already aroused, his flesh simply grew harder under her nimble fingers. "Your body wants mine too," she replied.

He stroked her intimately then, his eyes never leaving the dreamily erotic expression on her face as he traced the moist seam of her femininity with his fingertip.

She shuddered violently, then gasped his name.

He kept stroking her, his fingertips growing slick with her essence as he slid them up and down the swollen folds of her sensitive flesh. "Unzip me," he commanded, his jaw tight with restraint.

She reached for the zipper even before he finished speaking. She freed him, aware that he was as hungry for her touch as she was for his, despite the night they'd just shared. She bit back a groan as he continued to tantalize her. Simultaneously penetrating and stroking her with his clever fingers, Michael fostered a seemingly endless cascade of sensations that streamed through her like a rushing molten river. Elizabeth quivered violently, her fingers still gliding up and down the thick column of his sex as she tried to catch her breath.

With any other man, she knew she would have felt awkward with this kind of blatant eroticism. With Michael, however, she felt pure bliss, intense desire, and the quiet pride of knowing that her body pleased him.

She circled his hips with her legs, edging forward until the swollen petals of her sex nudged against his jutting length. Shivering with excitement and anticipation, she brought him even closer, and undulated against him, her behavior startlingly, breathtakingly sensual.

Michael groaned. "I want you," he ground out through clenched jaws.

"Then take me," she breathed, still bathing him with the fiery essence of her sensuality. "Take me now."

"Here?"

"Here," she insisted, urgency in her voice because she felt too hungry for him to care about where they were or the possibility that someone might discover them. "Please, Michael. I can't wait. I need you."

Cupping her, his fingertips sank deeply into the core of her body. "You're ready."

She groaned, relief and pleasure in the sound as her eyes fell closed. "I think I'm always ready where you're concerned."

"Don't feel alone," he muttered as he bent to her, his lips catching her subsequent murmurings of pleasure and desire.

Elizabeth trembled when he withdrew his hand. "We must be crazy."

"There's nothing crazy about this," he insisted.

As if to prove his point, he placed his hands at her waist, lifted her, and brought her forward. He slowly lowered her onto his pulsating shaft, the shudders of her interior body like the aftershocks of an earthquake as she sank down over him. She purred his name, and Michael knew that if his heart stopped beating in the next few minutes, he would die a happy man.

Elizabeth rocked atop him, her body a snug vise around his maleness. Her breath flowed hotly against his neck, and her breasts brushed across his chest as she swayed back and forth, her nipples tight little daggers of pure sensation. She closed her eyes, her head lolling to the side as she succumbed to the sensuality of their joining.

"Look at me," Michael urged raggedly. "I want to see your face."

Elizabeth met his gaze, her heart in her eyes, all her emotions utterly transparent. Stunned by what he saw, he instinctively surged upward, his hunger for her passion and love excruciating as he buried himself as deeply as he could within her body. She answered his thrusts with repeated downward motions of her hips.

Their pace quickened. Attuned now to Elizabeth's needs and responses, he felt the telltale tightening that warned of her highly aroused state. He raced with her, reaching down, touching her, seducing her, catapulting her forward into an abyss from which there would be no rescue. She gasped, and he felt her start to spin out of control.

Michael kissed her as she climaxed, her body splintering around him, tugging at him, relentlessly milking him. The force of her release made a joke of his control, and he surrendered to the inevitable. He exploded in the next heartbeat, Elizabeth's name a guttural sound that passed his lips as he spent himself within the confines of her quivering body.

Still slumped against Michael a little while later, she opened her eyes and discovered that a new day was upon them. She stirred, smothering a yawn as she straightened and looked at him. He smoothed a lock of hair away from her cheek before he helped her to her feet, arranged their clothing, and then brought her up against his broad chest. He carried her to the bedroom after a quick stop in the bathroom. Once there, he gathered her into his arms, pulled a sheet over their naked bodies, and held her while she slept.

His conscience, even more vocal now, refused to let him sleep peacefully. It hammered at him, a relentlessly unceasing voice that told him he was a fool to jeopardize this woman's love and trust in the name of ambition. He finally believed the voice, and he decided against pursuing the documentary.

It wasn't until they bathed several hours later that Michael noticed the fingerprint bruises he'd left at her waist and hips during their lovemaking. Because he insisted on doing some sort of penance for marring her skin, Elizabeth let him give each spot an openmouthed kiss before she pounced on him with renewed sensual energy.

Michael savored the emotional and physical intimacy they shared in the days that followed. They made love, slept when their bodies gave out on them, shopped and shared the cooking, and then made love some more. They told each other funny jokes, watched videos, and took long walks on the beach late at night. They talked as well, about her family, allowing her an outlet for her distress over the continued estrangment.

Elizabeth's smile, the richness of her laughter, and her ability to express her love in a thousand different ways began a healing process in Michael's very battered heart, but it did nothing to ease his troubled conscience. She had a right to know just what kind of man he was, and the only way she would know the truth was if he showed her the proposal he'd written for the documentary. If anyone had told him that he was on the verge of sabotaging their relationship yet again, he would have denied it.

"This is lovely, Michael," Elizabeth said, referring to the prestigious Laguna Beach art gallery. Almost a natural extension of the hillside above the coast highway, the building that housed the spacious gallery overlooked the Pacific Ocean.

"I'm glad you like it. A friend owns the gallery. He and his wife lost their home during the fire a few years ago, but the gallery survived."

"Are they here tonight?" she asked, her gaze flowing over the large number of guests at the gallery.

"No, which is rare for Ted and Jenny, but their eldest daughter is getting married this weekend, and the entire family's gone up to San Francisco for the big event."

"I worked the Laguna Hills fire as a part of a law enforcement exchange program," she told him, no longer reluctant to discuss that part of her life. "It was a rough time for everyone. Have your friends been able to rebuild their home?"

"It took them almost eighteen months, but they've managed."

"They must love each other very much."

Michael looked startled by her remark, but he said, "They've always seemed to."

"Human nature being what it is, a crisis generally does one of two things to a relationship. It either brings people together or it emphasizes their differences."

"The memory still hurts, doesn't it?"

"I'm no longer sad, just wiser," she said.

"You shouldn't have had to go through such hell."

She smiled up at him. "It's over, and I'm happier than I've been in a very long time."

It won't last, he realized. *Everyone's capable of betrayal.* Taking her hand, Michael brought her fingers to his lips and pressed a kiss to each tip. "You'd like them, especially Jenny. She insists that Ted isn't happy unless there's a disaster in the offing. He's an ex-jock who's wired for sound most of the time, and she's this unflappable Kansan who has seen him through the births of their five children, as well as the end of one career and the start of another. He calls her his rudder, and with good reason."

Elizabeth and Michael stood on the landing. She glanced across the interior of the building, her gaze shifting to the panoramic view afforded by a wall of windows. The artist's canvases had been arranged on a series of easels deliberately placed throughout the vaulted-ceilinged structure. Waiters circulated, offering the elegantly attired, affluent crowd canapes and flutes of champagne.

Michael guided her down a short flight of stairs and into the crowd, pausing often to introduce her to people who greeted him. She recognized several of the movie stars in attendance.

As they strolled from painting to painting a short

while later, she said, "You've been friends with Ted and
Jenny for a long time, haven't you?"

Michael nodded. "Since USC."

"Were you all scholarship students?"

He nodded his head, his amazement showing in his
eyes. "You're sharp, Miss Lizzie. Very sharp."

She grinned. "I do try."

He accepted flutes of champagne from a passing
waiter and handed her one. "To you."

"To us," she countered before taking a sip of bub-
bly.

Will there be an us? he wondered, a forlorn sigh escaping him. Her attention on one of the displayed
paintings, Elizabeth missed the sound and the melancholy expression on Michael's face.

"You're very quiet," he remarked once they'd completed their tour of the gallery and walked out onto the
patio that overlooked the ocean.

"Just thinking."

"About what?"

She met his gaze. "What I said before. I'm happy
when we're together."

"That's a two-way street, you know."

Elizabeth grinned. "I've gotten that impression."

"Michael!" a gruff male voice boomed. "I thought
that was you, son. How are you doing?"

Elizabeth smiled, recognizing the man who approached them. "Hello, Mr. Buckman."

Their visitor squinted down Elizabeth before he
withdrew his trademark cigar from between his teeth.

"Don't you usually wear a bathing suit, a whistle, and a pair of thongs?"

She smiled. "I used to when Chris and I were lifeguarding together, but that was a long time ago." She extended her hand. "Elizabeth Parker, Mr. Buckman. It's nice to see you again."

"I know exactly who you are, young lady." After briefly clasping her hand, his gaze shifted to Michael. "You're awfully quiet tonight."

Michael shrugged, but he felt wary. He knew that Hal was no fool, knew that he would make the connection between Elizabeth and the documentary, if he hadn't already. The shrewd look in Hal's eyes said he had. Michael fought the urge to hustle Elizabeth out of the building at top speed, while his increasingly more vocal conscience told him that he deserved whatever he got from the older man.

Elizabeth's contented smile as she looked at him prompted him to make an effort to sound normal. "I wouldn't think of interrupting. You two seem to be getting along famously."

"Careful, son, or I'll tell accounting to forget your name the next time annual bonus checks are printed up." Turning back to Elizabeth, he asked, "Is my boy treating you right?"

"He's on his best behavior this evening," she assured him, smiling.

Noting the proprietary tone of Hal Buckman's voice, Elizabeth silently applauded the older man's obvious affection for Michael. She also recalled how much his daughters loved him, regardless of his brash personality and smelly cigars.

Hal pretended to scowl. "He should be working."

Elizabeth countered, "He needs a change of scenery every now and again, don't you think?"

"I don't want him going soft on me," Hal cautioned.

Michael looked mildly amused by their verbal Ping-Pong game. "Shall I leave you two alone to sort this out?"

She laughed. "I don't consider my dates disposable."

"That's good to know."

Elizabeth smiled at both men.

"You're very relaxed for a man on a deadline," Hal observed.

Michael's response was prompt. "The lady relaxes me."

The lady in question glowed and laced her fingers through his. "As long as I don't put you to sleep," she said with her usual good humor. "It is not my ambition to become your personal tranquilizer."

She failed to notice Hal Buckman's blink of surprise, although Michael didn't miss it. Hal, an observant man, knew he had an aversion to being touched by anyone in public. At least he had until Elizabeth. Michael knew then that the old fox was busily cementing his conclusions about Elizabeth. Michael regretted that he hadn't been able to guard their privacy a little longer. He prayed that he wouldn't have to explain the proposal for the documentary in front of Hal and the hundred or more guests assembled at the gallery.

Hal peered down at Elizabeth. "Did you know that our Chrissie has given us another grandchild?"

"I'd heard that. Congratulations. You and your wife must be delighted."

"We are." Changing the subject with very little finesse, he remarked, "We haven't seen much of you in recent years, Beth. Where've you been hiding? I remember someone telling me that you'd become a cop."

"Not any longer," she said quietly. "I'm a student again, believe it or not. At San Diego State. I decided to go after a master's degree in counseling this time around. I'm hoping to get into crisis intervention eventually."

Michael felt a surge of pride in Elizabeth. She was finding her way back to the profession she loved, but on her terms. He knew that speaking publicly about her plans was a big step for her.

Hal nodded, his gaze glancing off Michael. "And your parents? Are they well?"

Elizabeth's smiled dimmed somewhat. "They're traveling a lot now that Dad's retired from the force."

"Your brothers also decided to carry on the family tradition that was begun by your grandfather, if I recall correctly." This time Hal peered directly at Michael as he spoke.

"Your memory is excellent, Mr. Buckman. I'm impressed."

"Got a mind like a steel trap. Don't plan to let anyone forget it either." Hal puffed on his cigar. "How's the new project shaping up, son?" he asked.

Michael stiffened, but he didn't miss a beat. "I've tabled it indefinitely. *Dark Side* and some personal business are taking up most of my time these days. I don't expect things to change anytime soon."

"We'll talk," Hal said, his eyes confirming his belief that Elizabeth was the woman cop they'd discussed not long before.

Michael gripped his cane, his angular features a blank canvas.

"How's the ankle?"

"Great," he said, his tone terse. "The doctor says I can toss the cane fairly soon."

"Glad to hear it, son." Hal soon wished them a pleasant evening and departed.

Elizabeth sensed a vaguely discordant note between the two men, then told herself she was imagining things, but she knew she wasn't imagining anything a short while later.

Michael spoke only when spoken to as the evening unfolded. At first she assumed his attention had shifted to the documentary footage he was currently editing, thanks to Hal Buckman's less than subtle remark about deadlines. Many people approached Michael, the famous and not so famous. He made perfunctory introductions, then allowed Elizabeth to carry the conversations. She also noticed that no one seemed offended by Michael's behavior, and it struck her as odd. She'd never thought of him as temperamental until now, just iron-willed.

Elizabeth enjoyed the buffet set out by the caterers at the gallery—an exquisite veal picatta, sherry-laced risotto, a garden salad tossed with a balsamic vinagrette dressing, and an Italian confection for dessert. She suspected that Michael didn't even know what he was putting into his mouth, because his tension, which was obvious to her, increased with every minute that passed.

His silence wore on her nerves, but she didn't know how to help him while surrounded by so many people. She'd learned a great deal about Michael in recent days. She knew he instinctively buried his feelings, fiercely guarding them, reflecting, and then resolving alone the issues he tackled. He wasn't a man who trusted easily. Elizabeth felt fortunate that he'd begun to trust her at all. Certain that he needed time to think, she didn't press the issue of his silence even though it troubled her.

Michael accepted the keys to his Jaguar from valet parking, guided Elizabeth into the passenger seat himself, and an hour later they walked into his suite in the Buckmans' compound. He hadn't spoken a single voluntary word since their encounter with Hal Buckman.

Elizabeth watched him drop his keys and wallet on the bureau. He then set aside his cane, shed his sports jacket and tie, freed the buttons halfway down the front of his shirt, and rolled up his sleeves. He did all this silently and stoically.

Elizabeth held her breath when he paused and looked at her, not out of fear but out of despair because she didn't see even a hint of emotion in his eyes as he studied her. Her heart lurched painfully in her chest.

She reached out to him, but he shook his head, turned away from her, and walked out onto the upper deck. Leaning down, he rested his forearms on the railing and stared at the star-studded night sky.

Elizabeth didn't immediately follow Michael despite her concern. Instead, she shed her evening clothes, washed her face, showered, and pulled on one of his large T-shirts before joining him on the moon-washed upper deck. Then and only then did she express her worry.

"Talk to me, Michael. Don't shut me out."

As she stood at his side, she watched him bow his head and shove his fingers through his dense, dark hair. Something serious had happened, something she didn't understand even though it was clearly a source of considerable anguish for him.

Reaching out, Elizabeth smoothed her fingertips across his shoulder and down his arm. "Do you want me, Michael?"

He jerked his head toward her, finally looking at her, finally seeing her. Hope flared inside her as she waited for him to answer.

Exhaling heavily, Michael nodded. "I . . . need you, Elizabeth. I need you more than I can say."

ELEVEN

"I need you."

The agony in his voice brought tears to her eyes. She responded instinctively, doing this time precisely what she'd done the first time she'd heard Michael utter those three crucial words. She didn't judge him. She simply opened her heart to him.

She'd never been the kind of woman inclined to sacrifice herself on the altar of anyone's emotional distress, and she didn't plan to start now with Michael. She also possessed very few illusions about relationships, thanks to her former fiancé. What she did recognize was that Michael's admission of need signaled genuine emotional pain, not an attempt to manipulate her feelings.

Elizabeth viewed her desire to see him through the darkness presently shadowing his heart as the most tangible evidence of the depth of her love for him. She knew it would take him time to voice his feelings, so she willingly summoned her compassion and patience, even though she would have preferred it if he'd simply told her what was troubling him. Explanations weren't a prerequisite for her love, however. That she gave freely and without hesitation.

She studied him as they stood face-to-face in the semidarkness of the upper balcony. She wanted back the contented lover and confidant she'd known in recent days, but she sensed that it would take time and a lot of healing before he returned.

"Are you all right?" Michael asked.

Startled, she smiled at him. "You stole my question. Now I'm going to have to think up another one at this late hour."

He traced the curve of her jaw with his fingertips, then lowered his hands to her shoulders. "I should have taken you home."

Her heart sank, but she immediately rallied. "I think you already know where I want to be, Michael."

She felt both his tension and his tempered strength as he massaged the T-shirt-covered skin beneath his fingers. He searched her face with an intense but unreadable gaze, and Elizabeth couldn't prevent her sudden suspicion that he was in the process of memorizing her features. The thought unnerved her, because it implied that he wouldn't be a part of her future. She could no longer imagine a future without him.

"Let's go inside," she suggested, shaking off the anxiety coursing through her.

Michael hesitated, and Elizabeth sensed his reluctance even when he slipped his arm around her shoulders, but he did as she suggested. They walked into the suite, pausing once they reached the center of the room. Elizabeth gently deflected his hands when he attempted to draw her into an embrace.

"Will you trust me?" she asked.

He paled. "We wouldn't be together if I didn't," he reminded her, his voice as hard as steel.

She nodded, not minding his bluntness even though it still had the power to shake her at times. She knew he didn't completely trust her, but she also knew that miracles rarely happened in real life. If they did, then her family wouldn't have judged her so harshly, and her fiancé wouldn't have disillusioned her. She started with the buttons of his shirt once she tugged the tails free of his trousers. Unfastening them one by one, she pressed her lips to each muscular inch of hair-covered chest she exposed.

They could, and would, talk later, she silently vowed. For now, she tackled the first hurdle—forcing Michael to feel physically what he couldn't seem to discuss. Because she realized that he still viewed dependence of any kind as an unacceptable risk, she knew that his innate sensuality was still her most viable route to his emotions, and she would never apologize to anyone for seducing him as a means of helping to heal some of the damage done to him so long ago. If he didn't move beyond his past, they had no future.

Breathing deeply of Michael's unique scent, she pushed aside his shirt and savored the strength and resilience she discovered there with openmouthed kisses and roaming hands. She drew invisible designs on his skin with her fingertips and tongue, rousing tremors of response that rippled through his body as she explored him. She quickly grew feverish in her haste to touch him everywhere.

Sliding his shirt off his body, Elizabeth let the garment fall to the floor. The instant his arms were free, he reached for her, but she sidestepped him. Moving backward, she slowly drew the shirt she wore up and over her head, revealing her naked body to him with a deliberateness that was utterly sensual. With her arms raised above her head, she took her time as she turned full circle in front of him, inviting him with the erotic undulations of her hourglass-shaped body to savor visually what would soon be his to possess. She registered his body's burgeoning arousal when she paused, and she saw the strain in his facial features as she carelessly tossed aside the T-shirt.

Michael advanced on her. This time she didn't dodge his hands. This time Elizabeth walked straight into his heat and willingly surrendered to his touch and his need.

His hands roughly possessive, he tantalized her as he stroked her breasts, then drove the breath from her lungs when he plucked at the sensitive tips. Gone was the finesse of a practiced lover. These were the hands, she realized, of a man driven by an anguish he couldn't articulate. As she touched him in return, she wondered if he felt the desperation that drove her.

Michael's fingers roved over her responsive skin before dipping deeply, and without any warning, into the slick, tight channel of her femininity. She gasped, then exhaled shakily as he cupped her mound and tortured her with his exquisite touch.

"You're cheating," she whispered, shaken by both the streamers of liquid fire flowing through her body and his seductive power over her.

As he brought his hands up to her breasts again, Michael told her, "I'm allowed to cheat, especially this time."

Alarm raced through her. *This time?* What did he mean?

"With you, I can't not cheat," he confessed, his voice raw.

She embraced his proprietary tone, hugging it to her heart and banishing the anxiety of a moment earlier. She arched helplessly under his capable hands as he caressed her breasts. "I love it when you touch me."

"But . . ." he said, his expression intent as he repeatedly dragged his knuckles back and forth across her sensitive nipples.

She shivered. "I'm not finished with you, and you keep distracting me."

"You'd rather have me at your mercy?"

She answered his question by rising up on tiptoe to kiss him at length. As she stood naked before him a few moments later, her gaze settled on his groin. His arousal was too blatant to ignore, although hidden from actual view by his trousers.

"You would," he muttered, answering his own query.

She smiled as she nudged him back against the bedroom wall with her body, then molded herself to him like tendrils of wild ivy intent on circling the sturdiest tree in the forest.

Michael cupped her face between his hands and hungrily claimed her mouth, completely ignoring her earlier remark about distractions. She shimmied closer, her breasts pressing against his chest. She no longer cared that she was totally distracted. Elizabeth savored the taste of him as he plunged his tongue deep into the honeyed heat of her mouth and traced every ridge and valley he found there. Reaching down between their straining bodies, she blindly traced the length of his pulsing maleness with her fingertips before she cupped his loins with both hands.

He jerked under her touch, then throbbed against her hands so forcefully that she shivered in anticipation of what it would be like to have him buried inside her. Lifting his head, Michael sucked in what could be described only as a stunned, tortured breath.

Staring up at him the entire time, she unfastened his belt, released the single button at the waistband of his trousers, and then lowered the zipper that confined his maleness. He sprang free, the epitome of masculine strength. She clasped him between her hands, stroking his steely heat until her knees grew weak with desire.

"Now, Elizabeth," he insisted raggedly.

"Soon," she promised.

"Very soon, or I'll be permanently crippled."

She smiled at him as she eased his trousers and briefs past his hips and down his powerful thighs. Michael kicked free of his clothing, then dragged more air into his lungs. Resting his head against the wall behind him, he closed his eyes.

She flowed down his body like an endless swath of heated satin. Kneeling between his parted legs, she steadied herself with her hands at his thighs. With a simplicity that expressed her love for him, she took him into her mouth. She held nothing back, making love to him with her heart and every sensual instinct she possessed. She gave without reservation, selflessly and completely. She used her lips and tongue, sucking and kissing and licking until he trembled under her touch.

She literally blindsided him with her eroticism as she conveyed to him a few simple truths. No one mattered more to her than him. No one would ever love him more. His skin was hot and taut, ready to burst when she tasted the first droplets of his fiery male essence. Her hands resting atop his thighs, she kneaded the muscles tremoring there just moments before she cupped the twin spheres at the base of his manhood and gently manipulated them.

Michael jerked under her mouth and fingers. He groaned out an expletive that conveyed both shock and pleasure. His patience and tolerance abruptly ended. He drew her up from the floor, his breathing so ragged that he sounded like a winded marathoner. He embraced her, claiming her mouth before she managed a single sound of protest or approval. Looping her arms around his neck, Elizabeth sank into his sensual kiss and writhed against him.

He pulled her legs up, smoothing them around his waist as he readied her. She met his gaze, saw the incendiary expression on his face. His manhood nudged against the slick, swollen entrance to her body. She quivered in his arms, her body weeping for his penetration. He paused, though, and she thought she might go mad if he made her wait another moment.

"Please, Michael," she whispered brokenly, tears suddenly filling her eyes because she wanted him so much.

He shook his head, soothing her with fingertips that flowed like hot silk over her skin. "If I take you now, it'll be over before we've begun."

"I don't care," she said with a moan.

His strained laugh was his reply, but he won the battle of the wills in the end.

They began again, taking their time, deliberately taunting and tantalizing each other as they conducted their own ballet of sensuality. He teased and aroused her to new peaks, his fingers exploring, delighting, and then inciting mini-brushfires all over her body.

Breathlessly wild with need a short while later, Elizabeth finally begged him to take her. This time Michael answered her plea the instant she voiced it.

Reversing their positions, he pinned her against the wall and drove into her, a primal sound wrenching from him as he entered her body. He shuddered. She felt as though his maleness were buried in the very depths of her soul. He held her fast, repeatedly slamming into her. She gasped, clinging to him as he plundered her body and assaulted her senses.

Michael surged into her again and again, his pace more reckless than ever before. She answered each and every one of his thrusts with a downward twisting motion of her hips. The friction became excruciating, the most delicious thing she'd ever experienced. Elizabeth thought she would die if Michael ever stopped making love to her.

As Michael drove her closer and closer to the brink, Elizabeth grew frantic. She suddenly quickened deep inside, the searing heat and power of his flesh too much to resist in the end. She screamed his name as her insides splintered into a thousand particles of white light, a starburst exploding deep inside her body.

Michael followed in her turbulent wake, slamming into her with barely restrained violence until his climax shattered his insides and nearly drove him to his knees.

Clasping Elizabeth to his chest, his heart thundered as he staggered to the bed. They fell across it, landing in a tangle of perspiration-slick limbs, clinging to each other, both gasping for air and both stunned by what they had just shared.

Michael held her close, his embrace possessive and fierce. Feeling safer now, Elizabeth dozed off.

They stirred from an exhausted slumber an hour later, reclining against a mound of pillows and sharing a single goblet of wine.

Elizabeth spoke first. "Tell me what's wrong. I know something happened in Laguna Beach, but I don't know what."

He froze briefly, then spoke with jarring bluntness. "I can't talk now. Don't ask that of me."

"I have to ask, Michael. I can't ignore how upset

you are and pretend it'll pass. Was it something Hal Buckman said?"

"Hal just reminded me of reality, that's all."

"You're being deliberately vague," she pointed out.

He looked at her, a muscle ticking in his cheek. "Don't keep pushing me on this, Elizabeth. I'm not ready to lose you yet."

Shocked, she stared at him. "I'm not going anywhere, Michael."

"You don't understand."

"Help me to understand." Reaching for him, she set aside the wineglass and slid down beside him, molding her naked body to his beneath the sheet that covered them. "I love you, Michael. You're a part of my heart now, and that's not going to change. Not ever. Not even if—" She stopped.

"Even if? Finish what you started to say," he commanded.

"I don't need a dictator in my life," she cautioned, not willing to be a target and confused by his behavior.

A muscle in his jaw spasmed as he ground his teeth together. He finally nodded. "Finish, please."

She made herself say the words despite the anguish they caused. "Not even if this is our last night together."

He swore, the word crude enough to make her flinch. "I wish I could believe you, but no one is that committed to another person. No one," he said, sounding tortured again.

When she tried to tell him that he could believe her, Michael silenced her with a second onslaught of passion. Elizabeth gave in to him, but only because she felt the near-frenzied desperation in his touch. His refusal to share his feelings, not just the rawness of his emotions as he repeatedly made love to her that night, cemented her conviction that he truly believed their relationship was in jeopardy.

For the life of her, she couldn't fathom why.

Unable to sleep, Elizabeth left Michael to his restless slumber at dawn. She padded barefoot down to the kitchen, where she prepared a pot of coffee. Taking a seat on one of the rear patio chaises, she sipped the steaming brew, absently watched the sun rise, and pondered how to help Michael move beyond the roadblock he'd thrown up between them.

She recalled his willingness to become her emotional can opener at a pivotal moment in their relationship. He'd fought for her during that conversation, and she silently vowed to keep fighting for him in the same way. He'd forced her to deal with her estrangement from her family, not just the shooting incident. Thanks to their conversations, she felt committed to finding a way to heal the rift that still existed once her parents returned from their trip. She knew they would never comprehend the self-doubt that had prompted her decision to leave uniformed service, but she knew she hadn't lost their love. The love she felt for them would be her bridge back, she now realized.

She hadn't figured out how to help Michael when he unexpectedly appeared at her side a little while later.

Clad in shorts, an abbreviated T-shirt, athletic shoes, and gripping his cane, he looked ready for a walk on the beach. He also looked grimmer than a man on his way to a funeral.

Elizabeth started to offer to join him on the beach, but an abrupt shake of his head stilled the words before they could pass her lips. Heart thudding with dismay, she sank back against the chaise cushions and gripped her coffee mug. Studying him, she realized that the dark stubble covering his hard jaw made him look ruthless, not simply troubled. She belatedly noticed the stack of pages gripped in his hand. When he shoved them at her, she stared up at him. He dropped the bundle in her lap.

"What's this?" she asked, uncertainty surfacing inside her as she glanced at the handwriting on the sheets of lined notebook paper. Michael's handwriting, she realized, recognizing it easily because she'd seen some of the preliminary script notes he'd done on *Dark Side*.

"Read it. We'll talk later, if you're still here."

"If I'm . . . what is it, Michael?"

His expression fury-filled in the blink of an eye, he all but snarled, "It's what the man you think you love is capable of. You're living in a dream world if you really believe you know me."

Shocked, she watched him turn on his heel, cross the patio, and jerk open the gate that led to the beach. He disappeared from sight without another word, the heavy wooden gate slamming shut behind him.

Elizabeth started to read the pages that Michael had dumped into her lap. Immobilized at first by the contents, she scanned several additional pages. Her heart raced, her horror escalating with every passing second. The more she read, the more disbelief reverberated through her heart and mind. Her life and her emotions, her secrets and her anguish, had been put on display by the man she trusted and loved.

She couldn't believe Michael's wholesale use of information told to him in confidence. She'd trusted him, dammit! And he'd betrayed her by writing what amounted to the rough draft of a proposed documentary film. After setting aside the stack of loose pages, she covered her face with shaking hands and tried to calm herself. She couldn't believe that he'd captured her emotional anguish of the previous year with such disturbing precision, and she grasped now why he'd believed their time together would soon end. Damn him!

Although stunned by what he'd done, she managed to gather up her belongings from his suite and shove them into a small tote bag she'd left in the closet. She summarily erased every indication of her presence in his life, even going so far as to strip the sheets from the bed they'd shared. She walked home, her wounded pride and pain-filled heart fueling her footsteps along the neighborhood bicycle path rather than her normal beachfront route.

Elizabeth locked her door, unwilling to do anything but retreat from the world. As she numbly made her way to her bedroom, stripped down to the skin, and crawled into bed, she decided that Michael Cassidy would never again be permitted access to her emotions, her heart, or her life.

TWELVE

Michael walked up and down the beach for hours. His legs felt like lead-filled posts. He eventually stopped torturing himself when his body throbbed out an achey warning that he risked reinjuring his Achilles tendon if he didn't call a halt to his self-destructive pace. He also finally asked himself the question—did he want to spend the rest of his life without Elizabeth Parker? Unfortunately, he knew he'd waited too long to ask and answer it.

He returned to the compound, not at all surprised by Elizabeth's absence. He grimly observed that the only sign that she'd ever even been there was the neat stack of pages on the kitchen counter next to the unplugged coffeemaker.

He showered, but he didn't bother to shave. Hurriedly pulling on jeans and a gray polo shirt, he stepped into a pair of loafers, grabbed his wallet and keys, and departed the estate. He drove the short distance to

Elizabeth's cottage, intent on assuring her that he had no plans to direct a documentary that used her story, or any variation of it, as the premise for the project. He couldn't for one very simple reason. He loved her, probably as much as she hated him now.

He knew he'd lost her, knew in his gut that she would never love or trust him again, just as he'd finally, during his ceaseless walking on the beach that morning, realized that the risk of loving was far less daunting a prospect than the reality of spending the rest of his life without her. Elizabeth had taught him about real love, the kind of love that didn't addict, the kind that empowered and strengthened, the kind that nourished a heart gone too long without any form of nurturing. Unfortunately, he'd learned the lesson too late, and he'd harmed Elizabeth in the bargain. He prayed the harm wasn't permanent. If she was willing to listen to him, he hoped she would take him at his word when he vowed to protect her privacy.

After knocking for ten minutes on the front door of her cottage and getting no response, he made his way to Seagrove Park. He searched the beach and the commercial establishments surrounding the park, but to no avail. He even attempted to place calls to her brothers from his car phone, but directory assistance informed him that the numbers were unlisted. When he telephoned the published number for her pediatrician sister, he reached her answering service. He declined to leave a message, since he'd never met the woman and didn't want to alarm her.

Frustrated but determined to locate Elizabeth, Michael returned to her home. He'd thought of one last place to search as he'd driven up and down the streets of Del Mar, but as he walked to the oceanfront side of her property, he cautioned himself not to get his hopes up. He made his way to the rose- and fern-engulfed hideaway, even though he doubted that she would seek refuge in a place reminiscent of the intimacy they'd shared.

Although it shocked him, Michael found her in the gazebo behind her cottage. He died a little inside when he first saw her. Clad in a flowing black silk caftan, Elizabeth sat huddled in the canvas deck chair they'd once used as a lover's perch. Her slender arms circled her updrawn legs, her head was bowed, and her forehead rested on her knees. She looked dejected, alone, and alarmingly fragile, and he knew he was responsible.

Looking at her now, Michael realized he'd never loved or needed anyone more than he loved and needed Elizabeth Parker. He cursed himself for the hundredth time that morning, aware that he alone had caused her present condition, and he alone had tried to sabotage their relationship by forcing her to view him as ruthless and self-involved. He desperately needed to offer an apology, but he wondered if she even cared enough about him any longer to listen to the words.

He grasped, perhaps for the first time in his life, the real price for his lone-wolf existence. His entire world until then had reflected his aversion to emotional intimacy, but Elizabeth had changed all that. She'd made him want to be a better man, made him hungry for a normal life, even made him rethink the concept of a loving partnership.

Michael's heart froze in his chest when he heard the sob that tore through her. The shattering sound stabbed at him like a lethal blade. He died even more inside, because he knew he'd been the sole architect of her sadness.

Determined to set things right again for her, he said, "I'm not going to do the documentary, Elizabeth, so there's no need to let this thing tear you apart any more than it already has."

Her head snapped up, giving Michael a clear view of the damage he'd done. Stunned, he numbly registered the spiky wetness of her thick eyelashes, the traces of dampness on her cheeks from the tears she'd shed, and the shadows of fatigue beneath her eyes.

"Leave, Michael."

"I will, but listen to me first. I swear to you on everything I value in this misbegotten life of mine that I will not do the documentary. Please believe me." He turned, ready to walk away and leave her in peace.

"Why?" she asked softly.

He paused and turned to look at her. "I can't."

She exhaled, the sound sad and heavy. "Good-bye, Michael."

Her pain drew him forward, however, despite his promise to himself to leave once he'd said what he'd come to say. He stepped into the gazebo, but he paused abruptly when he saw her flinch. He told himself that he deserved to know that he made her uneasy at the prospect of being in such close quarters with him, but it hurt nonetheless.

"I'm not going to do the documentary," Michael vowed again.

Straightening, Elizabeth lifted her hands to her face, wiping away the tears clinging to her eyelashes before dragging her fingers through her thick dark hair. Silky tendrils bounced back into place to frame her pale features. "Why not? You're a man driven by his ambition, and we both know I can't stop you. Besides, we both also know that you have legal access to matters of public record."

Although unnerved by her big-eyed vulnerability, Michael found the courage to speak the truth. "Because I love you."

She laughed bitterly. "I've been loved by someone like you before. I don't need that kind of love, Michael, so keep it for someone you hate."

"I do love you."

She waved a dismissive hand in his direction. "Go away. Play your cruel game with someone else."

Now that he'd begun, he discovered that he couldn't stop himself. "I didn't want to believe that love could be unconditional. I was afraid to believe, Elizabeth. More afraid than you'll ever know."

"You're afraid to feel."

"But I do feel!" he insisted. "I feel emotions I never expected to feel. I didn't . . . I just don't know how to cope with it all."

"You betrayed me!" she accused him, that wounded look back in her eyes.

"I almost did. I wrote the truth as I saw it. I was going to make the film at first, whether or not you agreed. I can't now. I haven't got the heart to do it any longer."

"Do you have a heart, Michael, or is it just a chunk of muscle in your chest?"

Her words cut deeply, but he knew he deserved her rancor. "Yes, I have a heart, and it aches for you and for what you've been through because of me. My only defense is that I didn't know what my heart was for until I met you."

He winced when he saw her shock. A frown filled with suspicion followed.

Although an unfamiliar garment, he wore his humility with the dignity intrinsic to his character. "I love you, Elizabeth."

"How long have you known?"

"That I loved you?"

She nodded, looking as guarded as any woman in her position had a right to look.

He shrugged. "For a while now."

"And when did you know you wouldn't do the film?"

He gripped the entry post to the gazebo. "You aren't going to make this easy, are you?"

"Should I?" she asked, the shakiness of her voice more evidence of the emotional roller coaster she'd ridden that day courtesy of one Michael Cassidy.

"No, I guess not. You can do just about anything you want to me right now and get away with it. I'm not real proud of myself."

"How long?" she pressed, her stubborn side surfacing.

"I think I knew the first time we made love, but I was having trouble admitting the truth to myself. I'd never let anyone become that important to me, and I've never let anyone influence a professional decision."

"You should have told me about the documentary before we made love."

He nodded. "You're right, but as you've already pointed out, I'm an ambitious man."

"But I didn't think you were a user, Michael, until you proved it to me this morning. Does what I felt for you frighten you that much?"

Felt? He stared at her, remorse and regret nearly bringing him to his knees. He knew then that he'd lost her forever, knew then that the question he'd finally had the courage to ask himself no longer mattered.

"I deserve an answer," she said.

She did, but his emotional stress reared its ugly head. "Dammit, Elizabeth, can't you find a way to forgive me?"

She looked outraged. Michael floundered suddenly, not sure what to say next. "Can you?" he asked, but far less aggressively this time.

"I honestly don't know."

"Will you try?"

"This isn't really about forgiving and forgetting. It's more about trust."

"I know." His broad shoulders slumped.

She studied him for several silent moments. "A part

of me wants to. What kind of fool does that make me?" she admitted.

"You're not a fool, Elizabeth."

"Will you get counseling?" she persisted.

He nodded, no longer reluctant to confront what had nearly destroyed him. He knew in his heart that she was right. He didn't want to be haunted for the rest of his life by a fear of betrayal. Her love had allowed him hope, but he wanted to be free of the ghosts of the past. Sadly, he wanted Elizabeth Parker almost more than he wanted to go on living.

Smoothing her fingertips along the hem of her caftan, she sighed and stared at the Pacific. He moved out of the entrance to the gazebo. When she didn't voice an objection, he sat down opposite her. She finally met his gaze, but Michael saw only a pale reflection of the laughing, passionate woman he'd come to cherish. He hated that he'd caused her such pain. His heart constricted, reminding him of what he'd lost. Lover. Ally. Confidante. Friend. Elizabeth had been all those things and so much more, but he had very little optimism that she would ever risk her emotions with him beyond a casual friendship, if that.

"Talk to me," he urged. "I can handle your anger, because I know I deserve it, but silence is a deadly weapon."

She returned her gaze to him. "I didn't think anyone really understood how I felt last year . . . how I still feel at times when I remember that night at the bank."

Her shifted focus startled him, but he went with it. "It's impossible to miss. It's in your eyes when you talk about the shooting."

"But you're the only one who sees it. And you don't pass judgment or begrudge me the right to feel what I'm feeling." She paused, searching his facial features. "We've both been plagued by self-doubt, although for different reasons. It seems we both still have work to do on ourselves, Michael."

A stillness rooted in hope settled over him. Something in her voice told him that she hadn't decided to shut him completely out of her life. He didn't care why. He just cared that she hadn't asked him to leave. "What are you trying to say?"

Her voice sounded less fragile as she spoke. "You really do understand. I don't know how or why, but you understand the emotions I experienced, and you understand me. What you did shocked and hurt me at first. I felt betrayed, but those twenty pages you wrote made me think, once I started to calm down. They made me step beyond my initial certainty that your career was more important to you than the bond we have between us. Once I did, I started thinking about your intent, about why you'd done it in the first place, and whether or not it had the potential of being a part of a healing process for others, not just me."

"You didn't hold back when we discussed the shooting. You told me how you felt," he reminded her, hope that he hadn't completely lost her firmly rooting itself deep within his soul. "I paid attention, and then I wrote the damn thing because it was the only connection I had to you when we were apart for those ten days."

"But you heard what I couldn't say. You made sense of my emotions when I couldn't. You knew which words to use. You understood what my family refused to understand. I realize now that we're both guilty of not wanting to take risks, although for different reasons."

He agreed with her. "Conceptualizing is what I do, Elizabeth. I've had years of practice."

"It's a gift. You're gifted."

How in God's name, he wondered, could she praise him after what he'd almost done to her? His jaw worked. It took him a few moments to reclaim his composure. "I abused the gift, and I abused your trust."

She shook her head. "I'm not so sure any longer." Elizabeth extended her hand to him. "I'm not at all sure, Michael."

He reached back, and he felt the trembling of her fingers when he closed his hand around them. He longed to draw her into his arms, but he knew not to push his luck, so he contented himself with holding her hand. "I didn't want to hurt you. That wasn't my intent."

"The only time you've ever really hurt me is when you've put walls around your heart."

"You've torn them down."

She shook her head. "No, Michael, you're wrong.

I've simply helped you begin the process. It's up to you to finish the job."

"We both know I have limits to what I can tolerate."

"Then you'll have to push the limits back, because the only limitations you have are the ones you place on yourself." She smiled faintly. "Eleanor Roosevelt said that, and she was right."

The old Michael bristled. "I like my life. I'm in the driver's seat."

Elizabeth nodded. "Of course you like your life. Being a loner is easy, isn't it? You don't have any obligations to anyone, and you don't have to risk your emotions."

Michael stared at her. He didn't want to imagine a life without her any longer. "It's lonely." He paused, felt her fingertips trace a tentative path across his knuckles. "I was lonely until I met you, even though I didn't want to admit the truth to myself."

"Would you say what you said before? I'm not sure I heard you correctly."

Michael knew exactly what she meant. Since this wasn't a time for games, he didn't play any. He simply spoke from his heart. "I love you, Elizabeth Parker."

Tears brimmed in her eyes. "When did you ask yourself the question?"

Shocked by her insight, he answered her nonetheless. "Too late. Much too late."

Her expression gentled. "But you finally asked it, didn't you?"

"Yes." He found unexpected courage in her understanding. "I've loved you from the very beginning. I think I knew you were supposed to be mine the first time I saw you."

"That first night on the beach?"

"Yes."

"I knew too," she whispered. "I was stunned, but I couldn't stay away from you. I was so afraid you'd leave one day without saying a word to me."

"I should have been back in L.A. last week, but I couldn't leave. I've been a real idiot."

She smiled at him. "I agree, but mostly because you're worried about being abandoned if you let yourself love anyone."

He looked at her, humbled and unable to speak for a moment because she amazed him with the depths of her compassion.

"You're staring, Michael. Why?"

"Because I can't believe you're real some of the time."

"I'm very real and quite flawed, but you know that."

"You're fragile too."

Her chin wobbled. "Only when I trust."

"What about when you love?"

She sighed. "Then too."

"Could you ever trust me again with your heart?"

She shook her head, a chagrined look on her face. "I think I'd better try, because your name's already on the deed. I just hope you're planning to take good care of it."

He slid down onto one knee in front of her. Taking

both her hands, Michael vowed, "I'll guard your heart with my life if you'll marry me."

Elizabeth's eyes flared wide with surprise, but she didn't say anything right away. She exhaled, instead, the sound shaky. "I want you to make the film."

He shook his head, momentarily distracted from the fact that she hadn't responded to his proposal. "I can't. I won't put you through that kind of hell again."

"It has to be made. The public needs to understand how tough it is for people in law enforcement when they have to make split-second life-or-death choices. Just think of the lives that might be saved."

"You'd have to be involved," he cautioned. "I couldn't even attempt it without you."

"I understand, and I'm willing to try, but only if you're beside me every step of the way."

"It means reliving the event, over and over again. Nothing's sacred when a film is being shot. The media will be around as well. It can be a rugged experience."

"You'd help me?"

"You'll trip over me every time you take a step," he vowed.

"Then we'll do it together," she announced as she leaned forward and pressed a kiss to his lips. "Together we can do anything."

He caught her before she straightened with his hand at her neck. He curved his fingers against the warmth of her skin, felt the silk of her dark hair dance across the tops of his knuckles. "My knee's killing me, woman."

She grinned at him. "Then get up."

"I can't."

"Why can't you?"

He scowled at her. "You know why, Elizabeth, so quit tormenting me."

"A little humility is good for the soul."

His scowl intensified.

"Ask me again, then."

"Will you marry me?"

"Yes, Michael, but only if you accept a condition," she said.

"Anything."

"Swear to me right now that you'll never try to sabotage our love for each other."

"I swear, but I'll need help to keep that promise."

"I'll help you, and I'll marry you."

He surged to his feet, then drew Elizabeth out of her chair. He embraced her, love and passion and amazement unfurling within his heart. Her silk caftan swirled around their legs as he took her mouth and restaked his claim on her. He knew in his heart that she was the only woman he would ever love or trust. When he finally raised his head, he asked, "Why did you say yes?"

She looked up at him, sudden emotion filling her eyes with unshed tears of joy. "You already know how much I love you," she said.

He nodded. "But I'd like to hear it at least ten times a day for the rest of our lives."

"I can do that."

Michael studied her, his expression sober. He knew

her well enough to realize that she had something else to say. "There's more, isn't there?"

Elizabeth smiled tenderly. "Your heart isn't forbidden territory any longer, and it never will be again because you're willing to love and be loved. We have a real future now, a future we can share forever."

"Forever," Michael said as he leaned down to seal their love with a kiss.

THE EDITORS' CORNER

When renowned psychic Fiona hosts a special radio call-in show promising to reveal the perfect woman for the man who won't commit, four listeners' lives are forever changed. So begins our AMERICAN BACHELORS romances next month! You'll be captivated by these red, white, and blue hunks who are exactly the kind of men your mother warned you about. Each one knows just the right moves to seduce, dazzle, and entice, and it will take the most bewitching of heroines to conquer our sexy heroes' resistant hearts. But with the help of destiny and passion, these die-hard AMERICAN BACHELORS won't be single much longer.

Riley Morse creates a sizzling tale of everlasting love in **KISS OF FIRE**, LOVESWEPT #766. He'd been warned—and tempted—by the mysterious promise that his fate was linked to a lady whose caress would strike sparks, but Dr. Dayton Westfield knows that playing with fire is his only hope! When Adrienne Bellew enters his lab, he feels the heat of her need in his blood—and answers it with insatiable hunger. Weaving the tantalizing mysteries of a woman's sensual power with the fierce passion of a man who'd give anything to believe in the impossible, Riley Morse presents this fabulous follow-up to her sensational Loveswept debut.

Victoria Leigh turns up the heat in this breathlessly sexy, faster-than-a-bullet story of love on the run, **NIGHT OF THE HAWK,** LOVESWEPT #767. She'd pointed a gun at his head, yet never fired the weapon—but Hawk believes the woman must have been hired to kill him! Angela Ferguson bravely insists she knows nothing, no matter how dark his threats, but even her innocence won't save her from the violence that shadows his haunted eyes. When a renegade with vengeance on his mind meets a feisty heroine who's more than his match, be prepared for anything—Victoria Leigh always packs a passionate punch.

THRILL OF THE CHASE, LOVESWEPT #768, showcases the playful, witty, and very sexy writing of Maris Soule. He's a heartbreaker, a hunk whose sex appeal is hard to ignore, but Peggi Barnett is tired of men who thrill to the chase, then never seem willing to catch what they've pursued! Cameron Slater is gorgeous, charming, and enjoys teasing the woman he's hired to redo his home. He'd always vowed that marriage wasn't on his agenda, but could she be the woman he'd been waiting for all his life? When a pretty designer finds that a handshake feels more like an embrace, Maris Soule sets a delicious game in motion.

Praised by *Romantic Times* as "a magnificent writer," Terry Lawrence presents **DRIVEN TO DISTRACTION**, LOVESWEPT #769. Cole Creek is almost too much man to spend a month with in the confines of a car, Evie Mercer admits, but sitting too close for comfort next to him will certainly make the miles fly! Sharing tight quarters with a woman he's fallen head-over-heels for isn't such a good idea, especially when a tender kiss explodes into pure, primal yearning. Terry Lawrence knows just how to entangle smart, sexy women with an appetite for all life offers with the kind of men the best dreams are made of.

Happy reading!

With warmest wishes,

Beth de Guzman

Shauna Summers

Beth de Guzman

Shauna Summers

Senior Editor

Associate Editor

P.S. Watch for these fascinating Bantam women's fiction titles coming in December: With her spellbinding imagination and seductive voice, Kay Hooper is the only author worthy of being called today's successor to Victoria Holt; now, she has created a unique and stunning tale of contemporary suspense that begins with a mysterious homecoming and ends in a shattering explosion of passion, greed, and murder—and all because a stranger says her name is **AMANDA**. *New York Times* bestselling author Sandra Brown's **HEAVEN'S PRICE** will be available in paperback, and Katherine O'Neal, winner of the *Romantic Times* Award for Best Sensual Historical Romance, unveils **MASTER OF PARADISE**—a tantalizing tale of a notorious pirate, a rebellious beauty, and a dangerously erotic duel of hearts. Finally, in the bestselling tradition of Arnette Lamb and Pamela Morsi, **TEXAS OUTLAW** is a triumph of captivating romance and adventure from spectacular newcomer Adrienne deWolfe. Be sure to catch next month's LOVESWEPTs for a preview of these wonderful novels. And immediately following this page, catch a glimpse of the outstanding Bantam women's fiction titles on sale *now*!

Don't miss these extraordinary books
by your favorite Bantam authors

On sale in October:

BRAZEN
by Susan Johnson

THE REDHEAD
AND
THE PREACHER
by Sandra Chastain

THE QUEST
by Juliana Garnett

BRAZEN

by bestselling author
Susan Johnson

Countess Angela de Grae seemed to have everything a woman could want: wealth, position, and an exquisite beauty that had once bewitched even the Prince of Wales. But from the moment the dashing American playboy and adventurer Kit Braddock laid eyes on the legendary Countess Angel, he knew she was unlike the other rich, jaded blue bloods he'd ever met. For beneath the polish and glitter of her privileged life, he glimpsed a courageous woman tormented by a secret heartache. Determined to uncover the real Angela de Grae, what Kit found was a passionate soul mate trapped in a dangerous situation by a desperate man. And in one moment of reckless, stolen pleasure, Kit would pledge his very life to rescue her and give her the one thing she'd forbidden herself: the ecstasy of true love.

"How can we leave? Bertie's still here," Angela replied with a small sigh. No one could precede a royal guest.

Kit's eyes shone with mischief. "I *could* lower you over the balustrade and we could *both* escape."

Her mouth quirked faintly in a tentative smile. "How tempting. Are the festivities wearing thin for you too, Mr. Braddock? We were supposed to formally meet tonight," she graciously added. "I'm Angela de Grae, a good friend of Priscilla's mother."

"I thought so," he neutrally replied. He silently commended her for the subtle insinuation of the name of the young woman he'd been seeing lately, and thought her gracious for not flaunting her celebrity. She was a professional beauty; her photos sold in enormous numbers in England. "And yes, worn thin is a very polite expression for my current mood. I'm racing early tomorrow and I'd rather sleep tonight than watch everyone become increasingly drunk."

"Champagne *is* flowing in torrents, but Bertie is pleased with his victory. Especially after losing to his nephew last year."

"Willie deserved his trouncing today. He should have been disqualified for almost shearing off our bow on the turn. But at the moment I'm only concerned with escaping from the party. If I'm going to have my crew in shape in the morning, we're all going to need some rest."

"Do they wait for your return?" The countess's voice held the smallest hint of huskiness, an unconsciously flirtatious voice.

"Priscilla doesn't know, of course." Kit Braddock referred to his female companions as crew; reportedly he kept a small harem on board his yacht to entertain him on his journeys around the world.

"She's too young to know," he casually replied, "and rumor probably exaggerates."

The countess took note of the equivocal adverb but she too understood the demands of politesse and said, "Yes, I'm sure," to both portions of his statement. It was very much a man's world in which she lived, and while her enormous personal wealth had always allowed her a greater measure of freedom than that allowed other women, even Angela de Grae had at times to recognize the stark reality of the double standard.

"Well then?" His deep voice held a teasing query.

"I'm not sure my mopish brooding is worth a broken leg," Angela pleasantly retorted, rising from her chair and moving the small distance to the balustrade. Gazing over the climbing roses, she swiftly contemplated the drop to the ground. "Are you very strong? I certainly hope so," she quickly added, hoisting herself up on the balustrade and smoothly swinging her legs and lacy skirts over the side. "Although, Mr. Braddock," she went on in a delectable drawl, smiling at him from over her bare shoulder, "you certainly *look* like you have the strength to rescue us from this tedious evening."

How old *was she?* he found himself suddenly wondering. She looked like a young girl perched on the terrace rail, her hands braced to balance herself. In the next quicksilver instant he decided it didn't matter. And in a flashing moment more he was responding to the smile that had charmed a legion of men since young "Angel" Lawton had first smiled up at her grandpapa from the cradle and Viscount Lawton decided to overlook his scapegrace son in his will and leave his fortune to his beautiful granddaughter.

"Wait," Kit said, apropos her pose and other more disturbing sensations engendered by the countess's tempting smile. Leaping down onto the grass bordering the flower beds, he gingerly stepped between the tall stands of lilies, stopped directly below her, lifted his arms, smiled, and said, "Now."

Without hesitation she jumped in a flurry of petticoats and handmade lace and fell into his arms.

THE REDHEAD AND THE PREACHER

by award-winning author

Sandra Chastain

"This delightful author has a tremendous talent that places her on a pinnacle reserved for special romance writers."
—*Affaire de Coeur*

McKenzie Kathryn Calhoun didn't mean to rob the bank in Promise, Kansas. But when she accidentally did, she didn't think, she ran. Suddenly the raggedy tomboy the town rejected had the money to make a life for herself . . . if she didn't get caught. But it was just her luck to find herself sitting across the stagecoach from a dangerously handsome, gun-toting preacher who seemed to see through her bravado to the desperate woman beneath.

Assuming the identity of the minister had seemed a ready-made cover for his mission. Now, in the coach, he amused himself by listening, feeling, allowing his mind's eye to discover the identity of his traveling companion.

Female, he confirmed. The driver had called her ma'am.

A good build and firm step, because the carriage

had tilted as she stepped inside, and she'd settled herself without a lot of swishing around.

Probably no-nonsense, for he could see the tips of her boots beneath the brim of his hat. The boots were worn, though the clothing looked new. The only scent in the air was that of the dye in the cloth.

Practical, for she'd planted both feet firmly on the floor of the coach and hadn't moved them; no fidgeting or fussing with herself.

Deciding that she seemed safe enough, he flicked the brim of his hat back and took a look at her.

Wrong, on all four counts. Dead wrong. She was sitting quietly, yes, but that stillness was born of sheer determination—no, more like desperation. She was looking down at rough, red hands and holding on to her portmanteau as if she dared anybody to touch it. Her eyes weren't closed, but they might as well have been.

The stage moved away in a lumbering motion as it picked up speed.

The woman didn't move.

Finally, after an hour of steady galloping by the horses pulling the stagecoach, she let out a deep breath and appeared to relax.

"Looks like you got away," he said.

"What?" She raised a veil of sooty lashes to reveal huge eyes as green as the moss along the banks of the Mississippi River where he'd played as a child. Something about her was all wrong. The set of her lips was meant to challenge. But beneath that bravado he sensed an appealing uncertainty that softened the lines in her forehead.

"Back there you looked as if you were running away from home and were afraid you wouldn't escape," he said.

"I was," she said.

"Pretty risky, a woman alone. No traveling companion, no family?"

"Don't have any, buried my—the last—companion back in Promise."

Macky risked taking a look at the man across from her. He was big, six feet of black, beginning with his boots and ending with the patch over his eye and a hat that cast a shadow over a face etched by a two-day growth of beard. There was an impression of quiet danger in the casual way he seemed to look straight through her as if he knew that she was an impostor and was waiting for her to confess.

Across the carriage, Bran was aware of the girl's scrutiny. He felt himself giving her a reluctant grin. She was a feisty one, his peculiar-looking companion with wisps of hot red hair trying to escape her odd little hat. She had a strong face and a wide mouth. But what held him were green eyes that, no matter how frosty she tried to make them, still shimmered with sparks of silver lightning.

"I'm called Bran," he said slowly.

Bran decided she was definitely running away from something, but he couldn't figure what. He should back off. Planning the job waiting for him in Heaven was what he ought to be doing.

Bran had always found women ready to make a casual relationship with him more personal. They seemed attracted to danger. But this one didn't. And that cool independence had become a challenge.

Maybe a little conversation would shake the uneasy feeling that he was experiencing.

"What are you called?" he asked.

"Trouble mostly," she said with a sigh that told him more than she'd intended.

"That's an odd name for a woman."

"That's as good as you're going to get," she added, lifting a corner of the shade covering the open window.

Good? There it was again. "Good is a rare quality in my life." He took a long look at her. "But I'm willing to reserve judgment."

He was doing it again—extending the conversation. Something about this young woman was intriguing. "Truth is, I'm a lot more likely to appreciate a woman who's bad. Wake me when we get to the way station."

THE QUEST
by dazzling new talent
Juliana Garnett

"An opulent and sensuous tale of unbridled
passions. I couldn't stop reading."
—Bertrice Small, author of *The Love Slave*

*All his life, the notorious Rolf of Dragonwyck, known as
the Dragon, has taken what he wanted by the strength of
his sword and the fierceness of his spirit. But now his
enemies have found the chink in his armor: his beloved
son. With the boy held prisoner by the ruthless Earl of
Seabrook, the Dragon will do anything to get him back.
Yet when he decides to trade a hostage for a hostage and
takes the beautiful Lady Annice d'Arcy captive, the sea-
soned knight is in for a shock: far from the biddable maiden
he expects, he finds himself saddled with a recklessly defi-
ant lady who has a rather dangerous effect on his body
and his soul. Suddenly, the fearless Dragon wonders if he
might win back his child . . . only to lose his warrior's
heart.*

Uneasy at his seeming indifference to her presence,
Annice made no protest or comment when Vachel
brought her a stool and seated her between Sir Guy
and le Draca. The high table was at a right angle to
the other tables lining two sides of the hall, giving an
excellent vantage point. A fire burned in the middle.
Supper was usually a light meal, coming as it did after

evensong and sunset. It was still the Lenten season so platters of meat were replaced by broiled fish and trenchers of fish stew. Cheeses and white bread made up for the lack of meat. There was no lack of spiced wine, with cups readily refilled. Intricate subtleties were brought out for the admiration and inspection of the delighted guests. One subtlety was constructed of towering pastry and glazed honey in the shape of a castle complete with jellied moat.

'Twas obvious that the lord of Dragonwyck was not close or mean with his food, as if he did not suspect a siege might soon be laid at his walls. Any other lord might be frugal at such a time, fearing long abstinence from ready supplies.

Even the beggars common in every hall were being doled out fresh foods along with scraps; Annice saw servants burdened with huge baskets leave the hall. Frowning, she toyed with her spoon instead of eating. Was this show of abundance supposed to impress her with his indifference? Or had he already received an answer to his proposal, and knew he would not have to wage war?

Looking up hopefully, Annice noted le Draca's gaze resting on her. Thick lashes shadowed his eyes, hiding any possible clue, though a faint smile tugged at the corners of his mouth. He was too serene, too confident. He must know something. A courier could well have traveled to Seabrook and come back with a reply in a fortnight.

Her heart gave an erratic thump. P'r'aps she was about to be released. . . . Had negotiations been completed to that end?

She had her answer in the next moment, when he

leaned close to her to say, "I trust you will enjoy your stay with us, milady, for it seems that it will be an extended one."

The breath caught in her throat. One hand rose as of its own accord, fingers going to her mouth to still any impulsive reply. She stared at him. His lashes lifted, and she saw in the banked green fires of his eyes that he was furious. Dismay choked her, and she was barely aware of the intent, curious gazes fixed on them as she half rose from her stool.

Catching her arm, he pulled her back down none too gently. "Nay, do not think to flee. You are well and truly snared, little fox. It seems that your overlord prefers the hostage he has for the one I have. Or so he claims. Will he be so self-satisfied with his decision in the future, I wonder? Though I will not harm you, for concern that he might think it politic to do harm to my son, there are varying degrees of subjugation."

His hand stroked up her arm, brushing the green velvet of her gown in a slow, languorous caress that made her stiffen. One of her long strands of hair had fallen over her shoulder to drape her breast, and the backs of his fingers rubbed against her as he lifted the heavy rope of hair in his palm. He did not move his hand, but allowed it to remain pressed against her breast as he twisted the strands of hair entwined with ribbons between his thumb and fingers. Staring at her with a thoughtful expression, he slowly began to wind the bound hair around his hand to bring her even closer to him.

Annice wanted to resist, but knew that 'twas useless, even in front of the assemblage. None would stay their overlord. Helpless, she found herself almost in his lap, her face mere inches from his and her hands braced against his chest.

"It seems," Rolf murmured softly, his words obviously intended for her ears alone, "that your overlord regards me in the role of abductor rather than captor. Though there may seem to be little difference 'tween the two, there is a significant one. As abductor of a widowed female, I will be required to pay penance as well as a fine for taking you." An unpleasant smile slanted his mouth and curdled her blood. "Unless, of course, I receive permission from your next of kin—in this case, your brother."

"My . . . my brother?" Annice struggled for words. "But I have not corresponded with Aubert in years. We barely know one another, and—permission for what?"

Still holding her hair so that her face was unnervingly close, he grasped her chin in his other hand, fingers cradling her in a loose grip. P'r'aps she should have been better prepared. After all, it was not unheard of, though times had passed when it was common.

Still, Annice was totally taken aback when le Draca said in a rolling growl, "Permission to wed you, milady."

Don't miss these sensational romances
from Bantam Books, on sale in
November:

AMANDA
by Kay Hooper

HEAVEN'S PRICE
by Sandra Brown

MASTER OF PARADISE
by Katherine O'Neal

TEXAS OUTLAW
by Adrienne deWolfe

DON'T MISS THESE FABULOUS
BANTAM WOMEN'S FICTION TITLES